The Cache Keeper

by Kathy Sattem Rygg

The Cache Keeper | Kathy Rygg

ISBN: 978-1-5233012-5-6

1. Fiction 2. Fantasy 3. Middle Grade Fiction

Printed in the U.S.A.
First Edition, January 2016

ACKNOWLEDGMENTS

Publishing a book is always a group effort, and I had a great group that helped complete this second book in the Crystal Cache Series. First I'd like to thank my trusted and invaluable critique group, the Fictionistas: Dawn Ford, Shelly Nosbich, Mary Pleiss, Jennifer Rupprecht, and Alyssa Stieren. Their feedback, guidance, encouragement, and friendship is so appreciated. Jennifer Rupprecht also served as my line editor on this book, and she did a fabulous job catching all those pesky typos and inconsistencies that seem to slip by during the writing and revision stage. I'd also like to thank fellow author Laura Hansen, who is always a champion of my writing. Zak Mitchell's talent for illustration helped bring the characters to life on the cover. Thank you to Phillip Chipping with Knowonder for his willingness to publish the books. And finally to my two biggest fans, my sons Jack and Peter, for their love and excitement each time they hold one of my books in their hands.

Chapter One

Dylan wiped the sweat trickling down his temples with the back of his hand. The sun hung above the mountains, frying the overgrown weeds in the empty lot. He read the geocache title for the tenth time: "There's No Place Like Home." *Very funny*, he thought. The cache was located on a lot with no house. One of his favorite parts about this treasure hunting game was figuring out the clues that helped lead to the hidden containers.

The GPS with the cache coordinates beeped. "You have arrived at your destination."

EJ threw a rock at the "For Sale" sign stuck in the dry dirt, and it bounced off with a metal clang. "We've spent the entire summer geocaching and haven't found any other crystals. How do you know they're even in Colorado? What if 4E Labs already has them?"

"They don't have them," Dylan snapped. He didn't need to be reminded that he had no idea where the other three crystal elements might be or what horrible natural disasters they might cause if 4E Labs got a hold of them. It was total luck he had found the earth crystal in a geocache. At least it was safe in his neighbor's house, and Tera was safe in California where she had been visiting her grandparents all summer. But she was coming back tomorrow. His plan had been to find the other three crystals before she got back. It was the only way to protect her secret—that Tera had the power to create earthquakes using the earth crystal, and she could even be a catalyst for the other crystals. But he had completely bombed out.

EJ threw another rock at the sign, knocking it over. "Boo-yah! Let's find this geo bad boy."

Dylan scanned the ground looking for any type of container—a wooden box, plastic cylinder, or waterproof bag. As he walked the lot in a grid pattern, EJ followed beside him, walking backwards while he chattered.

"I wonder what the other crystals can do?" EJ's eyes lit up with excitement. "Maybe the wind crystal causes tornados—or dust storms! I saw on TV a show about dust devils. They come out of nowhere, do a bunch of damage, and then disappear. That'd be cool. The water crystal probably causes hurricanes. We don't have to worry about that though. There aren't any oceans in Colorado. Now forest fires, that's a problem. We have plenty of those on our own, especially with all the dead pine trees around. The fire crystal has gotta be the best one. Can you imagine being able to control fire? I'd totally pick that for my super power."

Dylan paused from his search just long enough to scowl at EJ. His jabbering wasn't helping. Dylan turned and kept going.

"Dude, watch out for that pile of…oh, man. You just stepped in it." EJ covered his mouth with his hand, snickering.

Dylan grimaced as he felt a clump of something underneath his shoe. The neighbors probably let their dogs out and didn't bother to clean up after them in the deserted lot. But it hadn't felt squishy when he stepped in it. He lifted up his foot and crossed it over his leg to inspect the tread. Nothing was there. He looked at the ground where his foot had just been. It sure looked like dog doo, but it was still in a neatly formed pile.

EJ finally stopped laughing. "How bad is it?"

"Not bad enough." Dylan bent over to get a closer look. Something about it seemed wrong. He reached his finger toward it.

EJ grabbed his arm. "Are you crazy? Don't touch it!"

Dylan shook him off and poked the pile. It felt hard, like plastic. He scooped it into the palm of his hand and held it out.

EJ made gagging noises. "You are really twisted, you know that?"

"Look at it. Seriously, does that look like dog poop to you?"

EJ stuck his chin out, inspecting it from a distance. "Does it smell?"

Dylan held it under his nose and sniffed. "Nope." He closed his fingers around it and squeezed. It didn't crumble. He held it between his fingers and turned it over. The bottom was smooth and flat, and he noticed a rectangular line. He grinned as the familiar excited feeling surged through him.

"It's the cache!"

EJ looked at him like he was crazy. "Wow. The sun's really gotten to you."

"It's completely fake." Dylan slid back the rectangular piece to reveal a secret compartment. He held it up to prove to EJ he was right.

EJ snatched it out of his hand. "Unbelievable. You

found geopoop! This is like the greatest thing since fake vomit. I'm totally taking this home and playing a practical joke on my brother."

Dylan grabbed it back. "You know you can't take it. The first rule of geocaching is you leave the cache in place." He reached inside and pulled out a folded piece of paper. "Grab a pencil out of the backpack, and we'll sign the log." Even though he hadn't found a crystal—again—this was definitely the best cache he had seen. And EJ had a point about wanting to keep it. Dylan would love to be able to take it home and freak out his older sister, Jordan.

The boys scribbled their names on the piece of paper. The container was too small to hold trinkets, and Dylan could tell by EJ's frown that he was bummed he wouldn't get to trade anything. The promise of finding a cool baseball card or a coin left by another geocacher was EJ's favorite part of the game.

Dylan folded up the paper and stuck it back inside the plastic poop, leaving it where they had found it. Then they climbed on their bikes waiting by the curb and headed back through the neighborhood toward their block.

EJ rode ahead of Dylan. The playing card taped to his bike's back wheel tapped against the spoke with rapid clicks. It was the sound of speed. As soon as Dylan got home he was going to search the house for a playing card. He stood up on the pedals and pushed hard up the slight hill until he rode beside EJ. Then he tucked his head and coasted down the incline past his best friend. He smiled at his small victory.

When they turned down their street, Mr. Lyman

waved to them from his driveway where he was toweling off his freshly washed car. Dylan braked and pedaled into the driveway. EJ skidded to a stop beside him. Dylan frowned at the black skid marks left on the concrete. Why would EJ do that on Mr. Lyman's driveway when he was standing right there? And Mr. Lyman was way too nice to say anything about it.

"On another geocache hunt?" his neighbor asked.

Dylan stood up, straddling his bike seat. "Yep. And you'll never guess what the cache container was."

"Geopoop!" EJ beamed.

Mr. Lyman laughed so hard he put a hand on the hood of his tan hybrid car to steady himself. "Wait until I tell the guys in the geological society. They'll probably want to search for it just to see it with their own eyes."

"If you ever want to try geocaching, you can come with us." Dylan couldn't believe Mr. Lyman had never gone on a geocache hunt before, especially since he was a local reviewer who approved new caches online. "There are a lot of caches that are easy to find. No hiking involved." Even though Mr. Lyman was old, he could still get around.

"I appreciate the offer, Dylan. Maybe I'll take you up on it sometime."

Dylan wanted to ask if he could go inside and see Mr. Lyman's rock collection, just so he could check and make sure the earth crystal was still in the display case. Mr. Lyman didn't know about the crystal's power—another promise Dylan had made to Tera.

"Hey, it looks like Kari just got home from soccer camp. Come on, Fish."

"Okay. See you later, Mr. Lyman."

His neighbor smiled, and Dylan followed EJ down the sidewalk. They caught up to Kari in her driveway a few houses down. She was dressed in pink soccer gear all the way down to the pink Nike swoosh on the side of her cleats. Her curly hair stuck to her sweaty forehead.

"How was camp?" Dylan set one foot down for balance.

Kari took a gulp of water from her bottle. "Hot. What have you guys been up to?"

"The usual." Dylan shrugged.

"Any luck finding more crystals?"

"No, but we found something just as good." EJ stopped riding around the driveway. "Geopoop! A cache that looks like fake doggy dung. I gotta figure out how to buy one online."

Kari rolled her eyes. "That sounds incredibly gross and exactly the kind of thing you'd love. You have a seriously warped mind."

EJ smiled proudly and did a wheelie in place.

The sound of a large car engine caught Dylan's attention, and he turned to see a black Hummer making its way down the street. He recognized it as Tera's dad's. He breathed a small sigh at the thought of Tera. Even though they had either talked on the phone or texted almost every day since she left, it wasn't the same as seeing her in person. It was like sleeping without a pillow—it just didn't feel quite right.

The Hummer slowed down and Mr. Paine waved out the driver's side window as he turned into his driveway.

"When does Tera get back?" EJ asked.

"Tomorrow." Dylan and Kari said it together and glanced at each other. Kari and Tera were best friends, so it didn't surprise him that she would know when Tera was coming home. But he wondered if she knew Tera's plane was supposed to get in at 3:25 in the afternoon or if Kari planned to greet her the minute she got home—because he did.

"Hey, Fish, have you asked Mr. Paine if he knows about the other crystals?"

Dylan played with the brake handles on his bike. "Not yet. I haven't had a chance. He's either been in California or working at NORAD to keep an eye on 4E Labs. Tera tried feeling him out about it, but she didn't get very far. He always cuts her off and refuses to talk about the crystal or her kidnapping."

Kari crossed her arms in front of her. "I don't blame him. I'm glad the crystal is buried deep in the mine, along with that creepy kidnapper, Frank."

A bad taste gurgled in the back of Dylan's throat. He hated keeping the fact that the crystal wasn't buried a secret from Kari and EJ, but Tera made him swear. She didn't want anyone to know they had it, especially her dad. And even though he would have done anything to save her life after being kidnapped and trapped in the mine under Dove Mountain, a part of him wished he had done more to try and save Frank. Plus, he was their only link to proving that 4E Labs was behind it all.

Dylan heard a car door slam and saw Mr. Paine get out of the Hummer. Then he heard a second car door slam. His heart sped up for a second, and he held his breath as he waited to see who else got out of the car. He gasped as he recognized the tall girl with long brown hair who waved at him from across the street.

Tera was home!

Chapter Two

At the sight of Tera, Dylan couldn't control the smile plastered on his face. What was she doing home a day early? Why hadn't she told him? He left his bike on the ground and jogged across the street to see her.

Kari let out a squeal of joy and sprinted past him, her arms outstretched. She wrapped Tera in a tight hug, almost tackling her to the ground. "You're back early! I'm so happy to see you! Look at that tan. I'd fry if I tried to look like that."

Dylan stood behind Kari, waiting for a chance to greet Tera. Her skin was the color of honey, which made her eyes look a brighter shade of emerald green.

She smiled at him over Kari's shoulder. "Hey, Dylan."

He gave a quick wave. "I thought you weren't getting in until tomorrow afternoon."

"My dad wanted me to have an extra day at home before school starts on Monday. He wants me to be 'rested' for our first day of middle school. You know my overly-concerned father."

Mr. Paine unloaded her suitcase with a grin and walked inside the house.

Dylan stepped closer to Tera. "That's perfect. I was hoping we could hang out on Saturday, but now we can spend the day together tomorrow."

Tera bit her lip. "My dad wants me to spend the day with him tomorrow. There's a new exhibit at the science museum he wants us to see."

"Oh." Dylan shoved his hands in his pockets.

"But we can totally still hang out on Saturday like you had planned." Tera's voice sounded flustered.

"I thought we were going shopping for back to school clothes on Saturday," Kari whined.

"We can shop in the morning, and I can hang out with Dylan in the afternoon."

"But we had a plan." Kari wasn't giving up.

Dylan wasn't going to beg Tera to spend time with him. "No, it's fine. Whatever."

"But Dylan…"

"I said it's cool. We'll catch up sometime this weekend. EJ and I will find something to do."

"We can ride over to that new video game store that opened up." EJ rode his bike up and down Tera's driveway, jumping the curb.

"See? It all works out," Kari said with a grin.

Dylan clamped his jaw, grinding his anger between his teeth. Tera mouthed the word "sorry," and his jaw loosened. He knew it wasn't her fault.

"So, in case you guys have forgotten, my birthday is in a couple weeks," Kari announced. "My parents are throwing me a party for my entire family. Boring, I know. The good news is I get to invite friends, so you're all invited. The bad news is they want me to have a theme."

"What, like fairy princesses or something?" EJ snorted.

"No, nimrod. Like a western party with barbeque food or a fiesta with tacos and stuff. I think it could be fun, but I don't want it to be dumb."

"Too late for that," EJ mumbled.

"Well, then you don't have to come," Kari snapped.

"Oh, no. I'll be there. I never miss an opportunity for free food."

"I swear, all you think about is food. You're like a human pig."

EJ's face broke out into a grin. "Now there's an idea for a theme party. You could have a pig roast. A nice big juicy pig rotating on a spit over an open fire in the middle of your back yard. Complete with an apple stuck in its mouth."

Kari stuck her tongue out. "That's disgusting."

"Actually, it's not a bad idea," Tera said. "It could be a Polynesian theme. The girls could wear hula skirts and leis, and the boys could wear Hawaiian shirts. You could have a big pineapple tower of fruit and serve different types of fruit punch out of coconut shells."

"I love that idea!" Kari gave an excited clap.

"You sound like you've been to a luau before," Dylan said.

"A lot of people in California have been to Hawaii. My grandparents' neighbors have a luau every summer."

"Ooh, now we have something else to shop for this weekend—a dress for me to wear to my birthday luau!" Kari bounced on her heels. Tera glanced at Dylan, and he smirked at the slight roll of her eyes.

"The cool thing about Hawaii isn't luaus. It's surfing. You should have a hang ten party, dude." EJ held up his fingers in the form of a "Y" and shook his hand back and forth.

Kari chuckled. "You? Surf? I'd like to see that."

"I tried it once," Tera said. "It's really hard. Body surfing is easier."

"No surfing at my party. Just hula dancing. Can you teach us how to do it?"

"I can show you the basics. Just move your hips back and forth." Tera held her arms out at her sides and pushed her hips right then left. She moved them faster and faster. Kari mimicked her movements but wasn't as smooth, or as fast. "Come on, Dylan. You try it."

Dylan shook his head. He wasn't about to make a fool of himself trying to look like a hula girl. "I don't dance."

Tera folded her hands in front of her. "Please. Just one quick hula." She batted her long eyelashes.

"Fine. But you'll see why I don't dance." Dylan placed his hands on his hips and jerked his body left and right trying to stick out his hips. Tera and Kari giggled, and EJ fell on the ground, laughing. Dylan knew he looked silly and cracked a smile. He tried turning in a circle the way Tera had done, but half way around he stopped.

A car coming down their street caught his attention—a white van. As it crept at a slow pace, Dylan's heart sped up. Thoughts of Tera's kidnapper flashed in his mind. Frank from 4E Labs had driven a white van. This couldn't be Frank, but had someone else from the company come looking for them?

"Dylan, what's wrong?" Tera asked behind him.

"Get inside." Dylan's voice was almost a whisper.

"Why?"

"Hurry, go inside before they see you!" He turned and grabbed Tera's arm, pulling her toward her house.

"Dylan, what are you doing?" She tried pulling her arm away.

He glanced over his shoulder at the van, which was two houses away. "That white van coming down the street. It's 4E Labs. Don't let them see you!"

Tera stopped and craned her neck to look in the direction of the van.

"Don't stop and stare. Come on." Dylan tugged on her arm. Why was she wasting time? Was he the only one who cared about protecting her and keeping her secret safe?

Ding-ding. Dylan heard the ring of a bell but ignored it, still trying to force Tera inside. It rang again, and out of the corner of his eye he saw the van stop in front of Tera's driveway.

"Hey, it's the ice cream man," EJ announced. "A bomb pop sounds so good right now."

Dylan let go of Tera's arm and stared at the bright pictures of ice cream on the side of the white van. His relief was quickly replaced by humiliation. When had he turned into such a wimp? Tera hadn't overreacted, and she was the one who had been kidnapped.

"Are you okay?" she asked.

"Yeah. Sorry. I didn't mean to freak out like that."

"Thanks for looking out for me." Tera nudged him on the shoulder. "You want something from the ice cream man? My treat." She pulled a ten dollar bill out of her pocket and bought four bomb pops from the van driver.

"Make sure you get change," EJ called. "One time I gave the guy two dollars for an ice cream bar that only cost a dollar fifty, and he kept the change. Total rip-off."

"Thanks," Kari said when Tera handed her the bomb

pop. "I need to get home. I'll call you later."

"Yeah, I'm heading out too. Fish, I'll see you tomorrow." EJ ripped open the wrapper on his bomb pop and rode his bike one-handed across the street to his house.

Dylan tore into his treat. The cold cherry-flavored ice melted on his tongue.

"I almost forgot. I have something for you," Tera said between licks. "It's in my suitcase. I'll be right back."

Dylan sat down on the front porch steps while he waited. Drops of red and blue popsicle dotted the concrete as he struggled to keep it from melting in his hand. He shoved the bottom third into his mouth at once and regretted it right away as his brain froze with blinding pain.

Tera came out the front door and sat down beside him. "Here." She held out a small black pouch.

Dylan loosened the strings, opened the top, and reached in. He pulled out a clear crystal rock with a splotch of green in the center. It looked just like the earth crystal, but the green center wasn't in the shape of an upside down triangle with a line running through it.

"I saw it at a gem shop in California. Since you never got to keep the real crystal, I thought you might like to have this one."

"Thanks. It's awesome." Dylan did want to have it, but not because it looked like the earth crystal. He'd keep it forever because it was a gift from Tera.

"Sorry we haven't found the other crystals yet. I must have looked up hundreds of caches listed in California, but none had anything to do with wind, water, or fire."

"That's okay. We'll just keep trying." Dylan smiled, but he was starting to doubt if there really were three more crystals out there somewhere.

"The good news is my dad hasn't noticed any suspicious activity from 4E Labs lately. Maybe life can be normal from now on, and I don't have to worry anymore." Tera finished off her bomb pop.

Dylan wanted her to be right, but he didn't trust 4E Labs. He rubbed the warm smooth surface of the crystal in his hand. Right now he was just glad Tera was home.

Chapter Three

Dylan scanned the shelves at the new Game Goldmine store, wishing he was hanging out with Tera at the science museum instead of with EJ. After his gaming system was destroyed in their house flood a few years ago, he hadn't been that into playing anymore. The apps on his new phone were just as fun.

Dylan wandered over to EJ. "Find anything?"

"Nah. This place isn't worth it. Let's stop by the Mini Mart on the way home and get some food."

The boys left the store and grabbed their bikes from against the building's brick wall. Heat radiated off the blacktop and seemed to suck the moisture out of Dylan's mouth. A large soda sounded so good, especially orange flavored, which his mom rarely allowed.

He followed EJ along the sidewalk that paralleled the parkway. It would take them right past the Mini Mart then on to their neighborhood. They stopped at an intersection to cross the street. A blue sign on a post said "Dove Mountain ½ mile" with an arrow pointing in the opposite direction of the Mini Mart.

"Dude, is that the Dove Mountain?" EJ turned around in his bike seat and nodded toward the sign.

"Yeah, I guess it is." The sign caught Dylan off guard. He hadn't been back to Dove Mountain, or its museum, since he rescued Tera from the mine shaft last spring. The blue sign looked like any other sign pointing to a tourist attraction. But to Dylan the sign led to nothing but bad memories.

"I have to check it out. Think you could still get in? You have to show me where everything happened." EJ pointed his bike in the same direction as the sign.

Dylan panicked. He needed to change EJ's mind. "There's nothing to see. The mine totally collapsed. Come on, let's just go to the Mini Mart. I'm really thirsty. Sodas are on me."

"It'll take like five minutes and it looks like it's all downhill. Stay here if you want, but I'm going." EJ put his feet on his pedals and took off.

"EJ! EJ, come on!" Dylan slammed the heel of his hand on his handlebar. Why was EJ so stubborn? As he watched his friend ride out of sight, he weighed his options. He could go to the Mini Mart and wait for EJ, or he could follow him to Dove Mountain. He knew it'd take way longer than five minutes to bike half a mile and back, which meant he'd be waiting awhile. And EJ would give him a hard time if he didn't go with him. Plus, knowing EJ, he'd probably find a way to get into trouble.

"Fine," Dylan mumbled. He turned his bike around and pedaled after EJ, thinking the Dove Mountain would be more accurate if it had a picture of a skull and crossbones beneath it.

The road sloped down enough that Dylan was able to coast after a few good pedals. Tall, thinning pine trees lined the street, and the cool shade they provided were a welcome relief. He had a ways to go, so Dylan gripped the bike frame with his knees and let go of the handlebars, balancing upright in his seat. He sped down the quiet road, the air whipping past his face and the sound of his tires whirring against the pavement.

He rounded the corner and the road widened, opening into a gravel parking lot. Dove Mountain. As he slowed down his heart sped up. Everything looked just the same as he remembered it; the small one-story building with the word "Museum" across the top sat in front of the domed mountain. EJ's bike wasn't in front of the museum. He was probably already around back trying to find a way into the mine shaft.

Dylan pedaled across the bumpy gravel parking lot, kicking up dust. The sound of machinery equipment caught his attention. It grew louder, and as he rode to the back of the building, he saw a front loader by the mine shaft entrance.

"I knew you'd come," EJ said, pulling up beside him.

Dylan didn't say anything. He was trying to figure out what the construction was for. A pile of boulders was in the machine's scoop. Were they sealing off the entrance? Clearing out fallen debris from the earthquake? There was one good way to find out.

"Come on. Let's go inside," he said.

"Inside the mine?"

"No, inside the museum. I want to ask Mrs. Stevens about the construction." Dylan rode back to the front of the building and parked his bike next to the glass door.

EJ joined him. "Will the museum lady give us a tour of the mine?"

Dylan ignored him and walked into the museum. A bell above the door jingled. Seconds later an elderly woman walked out of a door marked "Employees Only."

"Welcome to Dove Mountain. May I help you?"

"Hi, Mrs. Stevens. I'm Dylan Fisher. I was in here a few months ago. I'm neighbors with Mr. Lyman. Do you remember?"

"Yes, I believe I do. Welcome back. And I see you've brought a friend."

Dylan nudged EJ, who was bent over a bin of rocks on the glass counter.

"Huh? Oh, hi. Yeah, we want to get into the mine."

Dylan glared at his friend. "What he meant to say was we were just wondering what's going on out back?" He didn't want to say too much because he wasn't sure how much Mrs. Stevens knew about what had really happened.

The woman shook her head and hurried behind the counter. "Those machines cause such a racket. But, I suppose it's a good thing."

EJ and Dylan glanced at each other. "What is?" Dylan asked.

"That somebody finally bought the mine."

Dylan's stepped up to the counter. "Who?"

"A company out of Wyoming. I'd never heard of them, but the previous owner said they paid a bundle for it."

Dylan wanted to know more. "Why are they digging it out?"

Mrs. Stevens shrugged. "They must think there's still something of value in there."

Dylan immediately thought of the crystal. "What do they think they'll find?"

"These mining companies have new technology that

can extract resources they couldn't get to years ago. The only thing that mattered to me was making sure they'd still pay me to run the museum. I have bills stacking up, and ever since my neighbor, Frank, left, I've been having trouble managing my finances. He used to take care of all that for me after my husband passed away."

Dylan's spine stiffened at the mention of Tera's kidnapper. He glanced at EJ, who had wandered to the back of the room and didn't seem to be listening. "What happened to your neighbor?"

"Apparently, he just up and left. Didn't even bother to say goodbye, which is so unlike him. I just hope he wasn't in some kind of trouble, poor man."

Part of Dylan wanted to tell Mrs. Stevens what really happened. He didn't want her remembering Frank as a nice guy, because he wasn't. Instead, he steered the conversation to the construction out back.

"How long have they been working on the mine?"

"For the better part of the summer. That earthquake we had a while back really caved it in. They should be finished digging soon though."

Dylan felt like someone had slugged him in the stomach. What would happen when this company found Frank's body in the mine? They'd have to report it. And it'd become public news, probably even wind up on TV. Then 4E Labs would know the mine had been dug out, and they might come looking for the crystal. When they realize it's not in the mine, they'll search for it. And the first place they'd start would be with Tera. She was in danger. Again.

"What's the name of the company that bought the mine?" Dylan thought if he had a name he could tell Mr.

Paine.

"I think I have it in my office. Give me one minute." Mrs. Stevens made her way back through the "Employees Only" door.

Dylan paced between the glass display cases running the length of the room.

EJ came up and blocked his path. "Dude, what's wrong? You're acting kind of weird."

Dylan stopped and stared at EJ. "Someone has to keep that company from digging up the mine and finding Frank."

"What does it matter? I'm sure he's worm bait by now. It's not like he's going to come back from the dead."

"Shh!" Dylan shot a glance toward the office. He didn't want Mrs. Stevens to hear them talking about Frank.

"Ohhh," EJ whispered. "I get it. You think they're going to find the crystal. Maybe that's the idea."

"What are you talking about?"

"Maybe 4E Labs hired this company to dig out the mine, just like they had hired Frank to get the crystal."

Dylan gawked at EJ. What if he was right? What if 4E Labs was behind the whole thing?

EJ's face lit up and he started pacing. "Yeah. That makes total sense. 4E Labs gave this Wyoming company the money to buy the mine and told them to dig it up to find the crystal. And when they find it, they'll try to kidnap Tera again. Oh, man. This is huge."

Dylan glanced at his friend. He hated keeping the truth about the crystal from him. But he couldn't say anything until he talked to Tera first. It was her secret to keep. Not his.

Mrs. Stevens came back out of the office, holding a white paper in her hand. "West Coast Environmental Research Corporation. Now that's a mouthful."

"Thanks, Mrs. Stevens. Come on, EJ. Let's go." Dylan pushed open the front door, sending the bell above it clanging into the glass. He grabbed his bike and hopped on. He put his feet on the pedals and pushed off, wobbling through the gravel parking lot.

EJ scrambled after him. "Hey, can we still stop at the Mini Mart on the way back? I want a cherry slushie and pack of powdered donuts."

Dylan didn't respond. He didn't have time for the Mini Mart. He needed to find Tera.

As he turned onto the street and rode away from Dove Mountain, he kept his head down. He didn't want to face the uphill battle that was waiting for him.

Chapter Four

EJ didn't stop at the Mini Mart. He followed Dylan the whole way home instead. EJ could be annoying at times, but it seemed like when it really mattered, he came through. And he had spent the whole summer geocaching with Dylan, trying to find the crystals, so that said something.

A few blocks from his neighborhood, Dylan realized Tera and her dad probably weren't home from the museum yet. But as he turned down his street, he was surprised to see an unfamiliar car parked in her driveway. It was a maroon four-door with Colorado license plates. He coasted into her driveway and hopped off his bike. The front door of Tera's house was wide open.

EJ pulled up beside him. "Looks like they're home."

"Yeah, but this isn't the Paine's car." Dylan glanced in the car windows, but the driver hadn't left anything behind.

"Maybe it's the cleaning lady's."

"Have you seen the inside of their house? They don't need a cleaning lady." Tera didn't have any siblings, and it was just her and Mr. Paine since her mom died a few years ago. Their house hardly looked lived in.

"Duh. Maybe it looks so clean all the time because they have a cleaning lady." EJ gave him a snarky look.

Dylan ignored the comment and walked up to

Tera's front porch. Before he could ring the doorbell, she appeared in the doorway, smiling through the storm door. She opened it and stepped outside.

"Hey, I saw you guys from my window. What's up?" She wore a bright yellow tank top and white shorts, and her feet were bare.

"We have some news." Dylan motioned for her to come close, and she followed him to the sidewalk. "We were just at Dove Mountain and saw a construction crew there."

Tera's brows furrowed and she crossed her arms in front of her chest. "So?"

"So, the lady who runs the museum there said a company bought the mine and is digging it out. They might find Frank's body."

"Well, they can have it." Tera's brown eyes narrowed with anger.

"I think the company's a cover-up, and 4E Labs is behind it. I think they're really trying to dig up the crystal." Dylan whispered the last word.

Tera's arms fell to her sides. "But the crystal's not…" her voice trailed off as she turned her gaze from Dylan to EJ, who was riding his bike around the parked car in the driveway.

"Exactly," Dylan whispered. He noticed EJ pedaling across the street toward his own house. "Where are you going?" Dylan called.

"Home to get something to eat. I'm starving. You wouldn't let me stop at the Mini Mart, remember? I'll catch ya later." EJ coasted into his driveway.

Tera grabbed Dylan's arm. "You have to tell my dad. If 4E Labs is really trying to dig up the crystal, he'll need to check into it right away."

"When you say 'tell my dad,' do you mean tell him *everything*?" Dylan hoped she was finally ready to tell him the truth about the crystal's location.

Tera looked him deep in the eyes. "Only what he needs to know."

"Oh. Got it." Unfortunately, she was still set on keeping their secret.

"And now's the perfect time. His boss is here, so you can tell both of them. He came into town last minute, and my dad and I had to cut our museum trip short." Tera's voice sounded annoyed.

Dylan nodded toward the car. "I was wondering who was here. Is it the Commander from NORAD?"

"No. His real boss. From California. I don't think it has to do with 4E Labs. At least, it didn't until now."

The thought of telling Mr. Paine's boss about 4E Labs and Frank made Dylan nervous. What if the guy was able to tell that Dylan was lying about the crystal being in the mine? He was a top military official and probably trained in interrogation. Dylan was a terrible liar. The few times he had tried convincing his parents he "forgot" about a test at school, his cheeks got hot, his eyes watered, and his neck broke out in red splotches. His mom called it "dishonesty disease," and he had it bad.

Dylan turned back to Tera. She didn't seem nervous at all. How was she so calm?

"Don't worry. As soon as my dad's boss finds out about 4E Labs, he'll put a stop to the construction. Nobody will ever find out the crystal's not in the mine." She gave a reassuring smile, then walked up the front porch and opened the door for Dylan.

Inside her house nothing much had changed. The walls were still plain white, and the front rooms only had a few pieces of furniture. There were now some pictures on the wall in the hallway though. Dylan stepped closer and recognized a younger Tera in a pink tutu and another photo of her buried in the sand on a beach. A third picture was an old family portrait with a much younger Tera between her dad and a woman who had the same emerald colored eyes and dark hair as Tera—her mom.

Tera went past him down the hallway, and he followed her to Mr. Paine's office. Through the glass double doors he could see her dad sitting at his desk. Across from him, facing the door, was a man with a round head, graying curly hair like a poodle, and rectangular shaped glasses. He didn't look intimidating like Mr. Paine.

Tera knocked on the glass, and her dad motioned for them to come in.

"Sorry to interrupt, Dad, but Dylan and I need to talk to you."

Mr. Paine stood up. "Oh? Come on in. Hello, Dylan."

"Hi, Mr. Paine."

"Dylan, I'd like you to meet Colonel Thornton. He's the one I report to about 4E Labs and the crystal."

Colonel Thornton stood up, leaned forward, and shook Dylan's hand. "Nice to meet you, Dylan. I've heard so many great things about you from Captain Paine. I owe you a big thanks for all you've done to help us out with 4E Labs."

"Sure. No problem." The temperature of Dylan's cheeks rose a few degrees.

"Dad, Dylan has some news." Tera gave him an

encouraging nod.

"Yeah. Well, EJ and I were on our way to the Mini Mart and decided to ride past Dove Mountain. When we got there, we saw a small construction crew moving boulders and stuff out of the mine. I asked Mrs. Stevens, the museum owner, what was going on, and she said some company from Wyoming, West Coast Environmental Research Corporation, bought the mine and is digging it out."

Mr. Paine frowned. "I didn't know anyone bought the mine."

"Dylan thinks it might really be 4E Labs trying to find the crystal," Tera said. Dylan was relieved she finished the story for him.

Mr. Paine addressed Colonel Thornton. "I haven't received any intel on 4E Labs activity, but that doesn't mean they aren't behind this. I looked into having the mine dug out after the earthquake to try and recover Frank and the crystal, but the excavation crew deemed it too dangerous. Seems strange an out-of-state company would suddenly buy a caved in mine that has been abandoned for years."

Colonel Thornton nodded. "Richard, we need to get to Dove Mountain right away. I want to find out the names of everyone on that construction crew and investigate this West Coast Wyoming company. We also need to talk to the previous owner and get copies of any paperwork involved. Looks like my fly fishing trip in the mountains just got delayed."

Mr. Paine walked over to Tera. "I know I promised we'd have lunch today, but I really need to jump on this."

"That's okay, Dad. Dylan and I can hang out." Tera

smiled at Dylan while she hugged her dad around his waist.

"Why don't you order a pizza for lunch? My treat. Let me get you some money." Mr. Paine and Tera walked out of the office.

Colonel Thornton approached Dylan. "You're proving to be more valuable all the time. Tera's lucky to have you around."

This time Dylan's cheek temperature rose from embarrassment, not nerves. The compliment gave him a boost of confidence, and he decided to ask the colonel about the additional crystals.

"Colonel Thornton, have you ever heard of the four elemental stones: earth, wind, fire, and water?"

The colonel shook his head.

"There's a theory that the stone of creation was made up of four separate stones, one for each element, and some believe these four stones actually exist as crystals. I think the crystal I found was the earth crystal, and there are three more crystals out there somewhere. Do you think that's possible?"

"Anything's possible, Dylan."

"I think 4E Labs is after all four crystals so they can create the original stone, but I don't know what they want it for. Maybe to control natural disasters so they can make money off it. Anyway, I've been searching for the other crystals all summer hoping they're in geocaches like the first one was, but I haven't found anything. Do you know of any other crystals the military might be tracking?"

Colonel Thornton studied him for several seconds, making Dylan wonder if he should have brought it up.

"Where did you hear about this theory?"

"I read about it in a book. My neighbor, Mr. Lyman, is a geologist, and he showed it to me."

"Does your neighbor know about the crystal?"

Uh-oh. Dylan hoped he hadn't said too much. "No, he doesn't know anything about it. We just talk about rocks a lot."

"I'm afraid I'm not aware of any other crystals out there. The earth crystal is the only one I've ever seen or heard of. It's an interesting theory, though. If 4E Labs was after them, I'm sure Captain Paine would know about it." He patted Dylan's shoulder and smiled. "But if you happen to find something, be sure and tell me. We wouldn't want it getting into the wrong hands."

We wouldn't want it getting into the wrong hands. A quick shudder shook Dylan's shoulders. That was the same thing Frank had said to him the first time he tried stealing the crystal. But the crystal was safe, and Mr. Paine and Colonel Thornton were going to make sure 4E Labs didn't get any further digging up Dove Mountain. But the military didn't know about the other crystals.

Anything is possible. Just because Colonel Thornton didn't know about them didn't mean the other three crystals didn't exist.

"I'd like to meet Mr. Lyman and see this book that talks about the four elemental crystals. Would you mind introducing me?"

Oh boy. Dylan couldn't say no, but he couldn't risk the colonel going to Mr. Lyman's house and seeing the crystal. He'd recognize it the second he saw it. "Uh, sure. Maybe he could meet you here."

"I need to head to Dove Mountain. I'll stop by your

house later and we can go visit Mr. Lyman together." The colonel walked out of the office, leaving Dylan standing by himself.

Dylan needed a plan. He had to get to Mr. Lyman's house and get the crystal out of the display case before Colonel Thornton got back. But how? He turned to leave the room to find Tera. Maybe she'd know what to do. He caught a glimpse of himself in a mirror hanging on the wall behind him. Red splotches lined his neck. The guilt had already left its mark.

Chapter Five

"We have a problem." Dylan told Tera about his conversation with the colonel the second after he and Mr. Paine left for Dove Mountain.

"Why did you mention the other crystals to him?" Tera sounded annoyed, and Dylan realized he shouldn't have opened his big mouth.

"I thought he might know where the other crystals are. And if you didn't insist on keeping the fact that we have the earth crystal a secret, then we wouldn't be in this mess in the first place."

Tera glared at him—actually glared. "*We?* I'm not the one who can't keep their trap shut."

Dylan didn't want to fight with her. "Look, just help me figure out what to do. Colonel Thornton is going to come back from Dove Mountain in a few hours and expect me to take him to Mr. Lyman's. I need to get the crystal out of there before he sees it."

"Just ask Mr. Lyman if you can have the crystal back. Maybe it's time you kept it hidden at your house."

Dylan considered the idea for a minute. "I can't do that. I made a huge deal out of Mr. Lyman keeping it in the first place. Maybe if we go over to Mr. Lyman's together you can distract him long enough for me to take it."

"And you think stealing it from Mr. Lyman is better than asking for it back?"

"I won't be stealing it. Just borrowing it for a little while. I know, we can switch it with the crystal you gave me. They look a lot alike. I bet Mr. Lyman won't even notice. I'll switch it back as soon as Colonel Thornton leaves his house. It's either that or tell Colonel Thornton and your dad we have the crystal." Dylan knew he was being totally unfair, but he was desperate.

Tera blew her hair out of her face. "Fine. We'll switch the crystals. But what are you going to say to Mr. Lyman when Colonel Thornton comes over? Don't you think he'll get suspicious when someone from the military starts asking questions about the crystal?"

Dylan shrugged. "That's the colonel's problem. Not mine. And as long as we switch the crystals, we're fine." The more he talked about it out loud, the more convinced he became it was the best solution.

"Are you sure you want me to be the one to go with you? I'm not supposed to be around the crystal, you know, in case I accidentally touch it and set it off. Maybe EJ or Kari should go instead." Tera chewed on her lip as she talked.

"No, I want you to go. EJ would probably mess it up, and Kari would have some complicated plan. I trust you. And I promise to keep the crystal away from you."

Tera's face softened. "Okay. Let's get this over with."

They left her house and walked next door to Dylan's. Tera waited outside while he ran in to grab the rock she had given him. It sat on top of the pouch on the dresser beside his bed. His sister Jordan came out of her room as he ran back down the hall.

"Where are you going?" she asked.

"Just hanging out with Tera. Tell Mom I'll be back later."

"So your girlfriend's finally home?" Jordan teased.

"She's not my girlfriend. She's just a girl. And a friend." But Dylan knew she wasn't just a girl or a friend. She was Tera. And no word could describe her.

Once outside, they walked down the street to Mr. Lyman's house. As they approached the front door, Dylan rattled off the details of the plan. "You'll have to figure out a way to get him into the kitchen for a few minutes so I can switch the crystals in the display case in the living room."

"Any suggestions?"

"He always offers to make a fresh pitcher of lemonade. Maybe you could help him."

"I'll figure something out."

Dylan rang the doorbell, and moments later Mr. Lyman greeted them.

"Dylan and Tera. What a nice surprise. Come on in."

They stepped inside the single story, dimly lit home. Dylan recognized the familiar smell of coffee and heard the sound of talk radio coming from the living room. It reminded him of his grandpa's house. Dylan missed him. Ever since his grandpa had died, Dylan considered Mr. Lyman to be his adopted grandpa.

"To what do I owe the pleasure?" Mr. Lyman smiled kindly at them.

Dylan froze. He had been so worried about how to switch the crystals he forgot to come up with a reason for their visit.

"Dylan has told me a lot about your rock collection, and I wanted to see it. I'm pretty in to rocks myself."

It made perfect sense. Dylan smiled at her with admiration.

"A fellow geologist, how lovely! I'd be happy to talk shop. Why don't I whip up some lemonade for us first?"

"That sounds great. I'll help." Tera gave Dylan a quick thumbs up before following Mr. Lyman into the kitchen.

As soon as the room cleared Dylan hurried to the wood and glass display case against the far wall. The earth crystal sat in the middle of the top shelf, its emerald green triangle in the center glowing lightly in the dim room. He tugged the display case door open, which rattled the glass. Dylan froze, hoping Mr. Lyman hadn't heard it from the kitchen. Luckily, Tera's voice seemed to hide any other noises in the house.

Dylan reached his hand in, picked up the crystal, and slipped it into the right pocket of his shorts. Then he took the black pouch out of the left pocket. He dumped the fake crystal into his palm and carefully placed it in the case where the other one had been. As soon as he removed his hand he realized there was a problem. The fake crystal didn't glow in the dark like the real one did. What was he supposed to do?

Tera's voice grew louder. They were coming back into the living room. Dylan closed the door and winced at the slight bang. Then he remembered the display case had a light in the top. He slipped his hand behind the case and felt around for a switch. He found it and flipped it on just as Mr. Lyman and Tera walked in.

"You're like a magnet to those rocks." Mr. Lyman

handed him a glass of lemonade.

Dylan took a quick sip and glanced at the case. Under the bright spotlight, the fake crystal looked just like the real one. At least Mr. Lyman wouldn't notice a difference—for now.

Tera joined Dylan in front of the display. She gave him a questioning look, and he nodded. "Your collection is great," Tera said over her shoulder. "Especially the one Dylan gave you."

He nudged her hard with his elbow. Was she crazy? Why would she draw attention to the crystal?

Tera nudged back. "He told me the story about the creation stone and the elemental crystals. Do you still have the book on that? I'd love to see it."

"It should be right here." Mr. Lyman walked behind the solid wooden desk and removed a thick book from the floor-to-ceiling shelves covering the side wall. "Here it is. You're welcome to borrow it."

Tera accepted the book. Dylan watched over her shoulder as she thumbed through the pages.

"Thank you, Mr. Lyman. I'll be sure to get this back to you once I've gone through it."

He waved off the comment. "No hurry."

A knock at the door filled the small room. "More visitors? This must be my lucky day." Mr. Lyman made his way to the front door.

Dylan kept his attention on the book. But when he heard a familiar voice echo from the hall, he turned toward the door.

"I appreciate your time, Mr. Lyman. Dylan mentioned you're somewhat of an expert on rocks."

Tera closed the book and hugged it to her chest. Her

shocked expression matched what Dylan was thinking—*what was Colonel Thornton doing here?*

"Hello, Dylan. I stopped by your house, and your sister said you were here. Captain Paine is going to take care of our business matter, so I left him in charge and decided to drop by." The colonel seemed stiff in Mr. Lyman's well-worn living room.

"Tera wanted to see Mr. Lyman's rock collection and borrow a special book. It's the same one I told you about." Dylan pointed to the book in Tera's hands.

The colonel nodded. Then he walked up to the display case and let out a quick whistle. "That's museum quality." He leaned closer toward the glass. "That crystal in the middle sure is interesting. Where did you get it?"

Panic pulsed through Dylan's head like a chant as he pleaded for Mr. Lyman not to say the wrong thing.

"That was given to me by a fellow geologist." Mr. Lyman winked, and Dylan almost collapsed from relief.

The colonel glanced at Dylan before turning back toward the display. Nobody said anything for several seconds.

"Well, we should probably get going." Tera's voice sounded cheery and calm. "Thank you again, Mr. Lyman.

"Any time. Oh, Dylan, before you go, I wanted to let you know about a new geocache I just reviewed."

Colonel Thornton turned around. "You're a geocacher?" He raised an eyebrow in interest.

Mr. Lyman chuckled. "Not officially. I'm just a reviewer. But Dylan's quite the geocacher. He keeps trying to get me to go on a hunt with him. In fact, I thought it might be time to finally give this sport a try. What do ya say, Dylan? Care to take an old man on his first geocache hunt this weekend?"

Dylan would have said yes to anything just to get out of there before Colonel Thornton asked any more questions about the crystal. "Sure. That sounds great."

"Colonel, it was a pleasure meeting you. Stop by any time."

"Thank you, Mr. Lyman. I'll do that."

As Dylan hurried out of the house, followed by Tera and the colonel, he worried about Colonel Thornton talking to Mr. Lyman again. He had been lucky this time. Should he tell Mr. Lyman about the crystal? He thought he could trust him. Tera would never allow it. But then, she didn't have to know. And if telling Mr. Lyman would help keep Tera safe, then it'd be worth it.

When they reached Tera's house, she handed Colonel Thornton the book.

"I'll let you know if there's anything to this theory about four crystals," he said.

"What happened at the mine?" Tera asked.

"We put a stop to the construction until we can find out who's behind it. And we will definitely find out. If there's one thing you should know about me, I always uncover the truth." Colonel Thornton patted Dylan's back as he climbed into his car.

The vibration from the colonel's hand travelled down Dylan's spine, repeating the man's words. *I always uncover the truth*. He thought about the crystal. Hopefully, that truth would stay buried.

Chapter Six

Dylan tried sleeping in the next morning, tired from a night of bad dreams about digging up bodies and being interrogated in dark rooms by faceless men. He rolled over and slid his hand underneath his pillow, relaxing when he felt the smooth surface of the crystal. He laid on his back and held the rock above him, turning it with his fingers. The green triangle looked suspended in the middle, like someone had placed a thin piece of wire there and molded the clear crystal around it. He was glad to have it back, where he could keep it safe. But he wanted the crystal Tera had given him too. He let out a heavy sigh. As long as Colonel Thornton was around, he couldn't switch the rocks back.

Dylan got out of bed and put the crystal in the black pouch. He took the Lego house he'd built when he was eight off his bookshelf, opened the roof, and placed the pouch inside. It was his favorite spot to hide important treasures.

After getting dressed and having a quick bowl of cereal, he texted Tera.

WHAT TIME R U SHOPPING WITH KARI?

AT 10. THEN WE R GOING TO LUNCH. CALL U LATER :)

Dylan knew from experience with his mom and sister that shopping and lunch usually turned into an all-day event. He texted EJ next.

U WANT TO HANG OUT?

CANT. FOOTBALL PRACTICE.

Dylan threw his phone on the table. The last Saturday before school started and there was nothing to do. His dad walked into the kitchen.

"Good, you're up. I could use some help in the yard. I need you to mow and trim while I cut down some branches from the trees in the back."

Dylan groaned and dropped his head. "Do I have to?"

"Yes, you have to."

"How come Jordan never has to do yard work? You're discriminating against her, you know. She's going to graduate from high school without knowing how to work a lawn mower."

Mr. Fisher laughed. "Teaching Jordan how to start a lawn mower would be as useful as teaching you how to paint your toenails. Even if you know how to do it, it will never happen."

"It's still not fair."

"Just get it done and then you can have the rest of the day to yourself. I'm sure you and your friends can come up with a fun way to spend your last couple days of freedom."

Dylan trudged into the garage and wheeled out the mower. When he was younger he couldn't wait for the day when he could mow the lawn. He used to run around the house moving the down spouts and then following behind his dad as he made perfect rows in the lush grass. But the excitement quickly wore off once Dylan did it on his own a few times. Pushing the mower up the incline in their front yard was a lot harder than it looked, and the scorching heat this summer totally wiped him out before he even made it to the back yard.

He yanked hard on the pull cord several times before the engine sputtered to life. The machine sent vibrations up his arms as he started his path along the sidewalk by the street. At the end of his first row, he noticed the Paine's garage door open.

Tera's dad walked out, pushing his own mower. He smiled, parked his mower, and walked over to Dylan. "Do you have a minute?" he shouted.

Dylan stopped and turned off his mower.

"I wanted to let you know what's happening at the mine, but I didn't want to tell you in front of Tera." Mr. Paine turned and looked back at the garage.

"Why? What's going on?"

"We stopped the Wyoming company from excavating further and brought in our own equipment. The other crew had gotten pretty far, so it didn't take us long—we found him. We found Frank." Mr. Paine gave a satisfied nod.

Dylan gripped the handle of the lawn mower to steady himself. "Did you find anything else?"

"Not yet. But there's still a huge pile of rubble to sift through. Are you sure Frank had the crystal with him when the floor caved in? Could he have dropped it somewhere else in the mine?" Mr. Paine studied Dylan, waiting for an answer.

"Everything happened so fast and the whole place shook so much, who knows where the crystal ended up." Dylan looked at his freshly mowed path to avoid eye contact with Mr. Paine.

"Well, hopefully we're close to finding it. The Wyoming crew said they didn't come across it, but they may be covering something up if they're truly working for 4E Labs. We haven't been able to find a connection yet between the two companies. At least we got to Frank before they did."

"Yeah. But how come you don't want to tell Tera about it? It might make her feel better knowing that guy is really gone." The thought of having to keep another secret, and this time from Tera, made Dylan's insides feel like a tube of toothpaste being squeezed.

Mr. Paine shook his head. "I don't want to upset her. I've seen the look on her face whenever I've mentioned Frank's name. I think it's best if we just keep this between us."

Dylan knew the look he was talking about, when anger flared behind Tera's eyes for a second and her back went stiff. The look filled Dylan with guilt because he hadn't been able to keep her from being kidnapped, and he hated bringing up anything that reminded her about it. But he hated keeping a secret from her even more.

Before he had a chance to say anything, Tera walked out from the garage. She waved at Dylan. "Dad, I'm heading over to Kari's. Her mom is taking us to the mall and then to lunch."

"Do you have your phone?" Mr. Paine asked.

"Yes," she said in an annoyed tone. "And I promise I'll check in with you." She stood on her tiptoes and kissed her dad on the cheek, then turned toward Dylan. "I'll call you when I get back."

Dylan smiled and watched her cross the street to Kari's house. He started the mower back up and began cutting another path in the grass. The rhythmic roar of the mower was soothing. Dylan did a mental check of what had happened in the last two days and what he knew. The Wyoming company had been stopped, and Frank had been found. The crystal was safe at his house, and nobody knew he had it. And when Mr. Paine didn't find the crystal in the mine, Dylan could say it must have been buried somewhere along the way. He'd just make sure not to bring up Frank around Tera. That way, technically, he wouldn't have to lie to her about it. He took a deep breath. Things didn't seem so bad.

He finished mowing the front and emptied the bag of grass into the yard waste can before heading around to the back. He noticed Mr. Lyman coming down the sidewalk, who went for a walk in the neighborhood at least once a day.

Mr. Lyman waved. "Morning, Dylan. You look like you're working hard."

Dylan attached the grass bag back to the mower. "Yeah, and I'm only half done."

"Do you have plans the rest of the day?" Mr. Lyman walked up the driveway toward Dylan.

"Not really." With all his friends busy, it was going to be a long day.

"Would you be interested in going geocaching? I thought we could check out that new cache I mentioned."

Dylan's mood perked up. "Sure. How far away is it?"

"Not too far. It looks like it's in Chatfield State Park."

Dylan knew that park. His family had been boating on the lake there. It was way too far to walk or ride a bike.

"I can drive us." Mr. Lyman seemed to know what Dylan was thinking.

"Really? That'd be great." Going geogaching in a new area sounded like a great way to spend a boring Saturday. "I'll ask my dad, but I'm sure I can go as soon as I finish mowing."

"The rest of the gang is welcome to come along."

"EJ's at football practice, and Tera and Kari are shopping. Besides, EJ and Kari aren't too into it. Tera's really the only one who likes to geocache a lot."

Mr. Lyman nodded. "That's too bad. I was hoping to talk to Tera and see if she had a chance to look through that geology book yet."

Dylan fiddled with the lawn mower controls. "Actually, Colonel Thornton has the book. After we left your house yesterday he asked to borrow it."

"Oh, really? It seems like everyone is interested in geology lately. Especially the theory about the elemental stones." Mr. Lyman cleared his throat.

Dylan didn't look up. "Yeah, I guess."

"Does the colonel's interest have anything to do with that crystal you gave me? And I don't mean the one that's sitting in my display case right now." Mr. Lyman looked at Dylan over his round eyeglasses.

Dylan was so shocked at Mr. Lyman's direct question, he just stared at him. But his neighbor's eyes didn't show any sign of anger.

"Mr. Lyman, I'm so sorry. I switched the crystals," he mumbled.

"You really believe that rock is the earth crystal, and you don't want anyone to find out about it, is that correct?"

Dylan nodded.

"I trust you have your reasons for not telling Colonel Thornton about it. And I've always considered the crystal to belong to you, so as far as I'm concerned, it's back with its rightful owner. But next time, all you have to do is ask." Mr. Lyman smiled.

Dylan gave a slight grin back. The scolding wasn't too bad.

"Go finish your yard work and come down when you're ready. I think you're really going to be interested in finding this cache."

"What's it called?"

Mr. Lyman's blue eyes twinkled. "Wind Beneath My Wings."

Chapter Seven

Dylan drummed his fingers on the edges of the front seat in Mr. Lyman's Prius. Without the roar of a usual car engine, it was the only sound in the hybrid car. His bike made more noise than that.

"My mom said to ask if you want to come over for dinner tonight. My dad's grilling burgers."

"I'd love to. But I hope she'll let me bring dessert this time."

Dylan shook his head. "Too late. She already made a pan of brownies. Double fudge." He liked having Mr. Lyman over for dinner. It made his family feel complete again, like when his grandpa used to visit them for the holidays.

As they drove along highway 85 toward Chatfield State Park, Dylan thought about the geocache title: *Wind Beneath My Wings*. It wasn't the first cache he had looked for that had the words wind, fire, or water in it. None of those had turned up any more crystals. But he couldn't help hoping maybe this time he'd get lucky.

"So, when did this cache get submitted?" Dylan asked.

"A few days ago." Mr. Lyman drove with both hands on top of the steering wheel. His eyes barely peeked out from under his floppy, fisherman style hat.

"Chatfield is kind of far away. I thought you just reviewed caches close by."

"This still falls in my area."

Dylan wondered what the cache title could mean. Usually it had something to do with the location of the container. But what if this one had more to do with what was inside, or even the cache owner? "Do you know who submitted it?"

"It should say on the sheet I printed out, but I believe the owner is listed as 'Mile High.'"

Dylan huffed. "As in the Mile High City? That could be anyone in Denver." The cache probably wouldn't end up having anything to do with the crystal after all. But at least he was getting to geocache in a new place, so that alone was worth it.

They turned off the highway and wound around on a road that eventually led to an entrance with a wooden sign that said "Welcome to Chatfield State Park." They approached a small park station, and Mr. Lyman slowed down. The park attendant waved them through.

"I come here enough that I have a season park pass," Mr. Lyman said.

"What do you do here?" Other than boat, Dylan didn't know what else people did at the park.

"I like walking the trails and looking for wildlife. You never know what you might spot."

He followed the road into the park and drove past a large camping area. RVs filled the grassy area, while families sat around grills and played Frisbee around the trees.

Mr. Lyman pulled into a paved parking lot. "Do you have the GPS?"

"Yep." Dylan took the device out of the backpack between his feet. He had shown Mr. Lyman how to enter the coordinates of the cache before they left. He got out of the car and turned on the GPS. "Basically we just follow this until we get to the right area. From there we'll have to search for the container."

After several beeps and flashing screens, the GPS brought up their location. Then it showed the location of the coordinates. Dylan stared at the two points on the screen. "What? How can we be so close?"

Mr. Lyman zipped his car keys in the pack strapped around his waist. "What's wrong?"

"According to this, we're practically at the cache already. Did you know where it was ahead of time?" Dylan knew there were plenty of websites that could tell you locations based on coordinates, but the whole point of geocaching was to find them on your own.

"Dylan Fisher, are you accusing me of cheating?" Mr. Lyman's voice sounded serious, but his slight grin gave him away.

"No, I just--"

"It's okay. As part of the review process I had to verify the location, so I knew it was in Chatfield Park. But I honestly had no idea I'd lead us right to it." Mr. Lyman sounded sincere, and it was his first time geocaching.

"Here." Dylan handed Mr. Lyman the GPS. "I'll let you take the lead."

"This is rather exciting, isn't it?" Mr. Lyman cradled the device in his palm. He turned in a half circle and then turned back again like he was trying to read a compass. "This way."

Dylan followed him across the parking lot into a

grassy field. A loud buzzing sound came from overhead. He looked up and ducked as a giant, red model airplane soared by. It flew into the distance, made a large loop, and then headed back in their direction. It made a pass over the parking lot before shooting straight up. It climbed higher and higher then dipped and fell into a nose dive. The sound of an engine trailed behind it. Dylan waited for the crash landing, but at the last second the plane pulled up and coasted inches above the ground before landing on the other side of the field.

"That was so cool. I've never seen a remote control plane that big before." It was as long as his kitchen table.

"There's an actual runway over there just for model plane enthusiasts. I've seen them buzzing around from time to time. It looks like we're going to get a good view of the show. That's right where the GPS is taking us."

Dylan grinned. "'*Wind Beneath My Wings*'. The cache must be somewhere around the runway."

"Well, then what are we waiting for?" Mr. Lyman pulled down on the brim of his hat, stuck out his elbows, and started speed-walking across the field, just like the older people who walked the shopping mall.

Dylan laughed and sprinted past him, not stopping until he reached the model plane runway. While waiting for Mr. Lyman to catch up, he watched a teenage boy operate a yellow model bi-plane. It sped down the narrow runway and rose into the air, wobbling back and forth until the pilot leveled it out. The boy pointed a square black box with a long silver antenna toward the plane. He used his thumbs to work the controls like he was playing a video game. The steady buzzing of the engine filled the sky overhead, mesmerizing Dylan as he watched it climb, loop, and dive.

Mr. Lyman finally joined him. "It's harder than it looks."

"I bet I could do it." It had been a while, but Dylan used to be pretty good with a remote control car.

The GPS in Mr. Lyman's hand beeped. "I think it's telling us we're here."

Dylan scanned the open field and runway around them. An orange wind sock waved a few feet to his right, but it wasn't something that could hide a cache. A round metal trash bin was to his left across the runway, but he was pretty sure nobody would hide a cache in garbage. What else was there? "Are there any encrypted messages on the cache listing?"

Mr. Lyman unfolded a paper from his pack. "Nope. Just the title and coordinates. Should we check the trash can?"

"I think that's taking the 'Cache In Trash Out' motto of geocaching a little far. You're supposed to throw away trash when you geocache, not geocache in the trash."

"It can't hurt to check it out." Mr. Lyman looked both ways down the runway then walked across.

Dylan shook his head, convinced it was a waste of time, but followed. When he got close enough, he noticed the bin was made from a dark green colored metal and looked like a mesh basket. It had four short legs secured into the ground. The center was lined with a black trash bag.

Mr. Lyman handed Dylan the GPS and peered into the open top of the trash container. "It must have been emptied recently."

Dylan's impatience grew. "Nobody would put a

cache in a trash can. It'd get thrown away." When Mr. Lyman didn't respond, Dylan thought maybe he hadn't heard him. But then his neighbor gathered the edges of the black trash bag and lifted it out of the can. He let it drop to the ground as he inspected the inside of the container.

"Hmm. I thought maybe the cache would be underneath the liner, but it doesn't look like it. I guess my instincts aren't as sharp as they used to be." Mr. Lyman reached for the black trash bag on the ground. The yellow bi-plane buzzed overhead, only a few feet above them. Dylan and Mr. Lyman ducked.

"Sorry!" The teenage boy called from the other side of the runway.

"Quite all right." Mr. Lyman waved back.

A gust of air from the passing plane had caught the trash bag and blew it across the field. Dylan ran to grab it and snatched it up. He turned around and walked back toward Mr. Lyman. As he approached the back side of the trash can, he noticed a gap between the bottom of the container and the ground that he hadn't noticed from the front side. He bent down to get a closer look and reached his hand into the space. His heart fluttered when he felt something hard.

"What is it? Did you find something?" Mr. Lyman bent down beside him.

Dylan sat back in the grass, holding a black cylinder that looked like a small thermos. "I think I found the cache." He smiled at Mr. Lyman and then unscrewed the lid. Tucked inside the aluminum interior was a slip of paper for the cache log and a geocoin. He took the coin between his fingers and gasped at the image engraved on the front—it was an upright triangle with a horizontal line through the middle. He knew exactly what the symbol represented. It was the elemental symbol for wind!

"Did we find it?" Mr. Lyman gave Dylan an expectant look.

"Yeah. We found it." Dylan rubbed his thumb over the raised gold triangle. It was the reverse image of the earth symbol. He stood up and handed the coin to Mr. Lyman. "It's not a crystal, but it must have something to do with it, don't you think?"

Mr. Lyman examined both sides of the coin. "I'm not sure. The elemental symbols are pretty common, especially if you're looking for them. But there's a tracking number on the back of the coin. Maybe that will tell you something."

Dylan took the coin back and looked at the tracking code. Maybe it was just a coincidence. He knew Mr. Lyman didn't believe in the crystals, but thanks to him, this was the closest he'd come to finding a clue. He needed to get home and look up the tracking code.

Mr. Lyman took out a pencil from his pack and printed his name on the cache log. He handed the pencil to Dylan, who scribbled his name, leaving off the "E" and "R" in Fisher. "There isn't anything to trade, but you can leave something in the cache if you want."

Mr. Lyman shook his head. "Finding the cache was enough for me. I'll bring something to trade next time. Assuming you don't mind if there is a next time?"

Dylan shook his head. Mr. Lyman could go geocaching with him any time.

Chapter Eight

Dylan glanced at the wind geocoin every ten seconds. Mr. Lyman had placed it in the center console of his car for the ride home. Was he going to let Dylan have it, or was his neighbor going to hang on to it until they went geocaching again? He hadn't said anything since they found it, and Dylan really wanted to look up the tracking code when he got home. He should just ask Mr. Lyman if he could have it, but the words wouldn't come out of his mouth.

They pulled into his driveway, and Dylan pretended to fumble with his seatbelt. He took his time gathering his backpack and paused after opening the car door. "Thanks for driving, Mr. Lyman. That was a lot of fun."

"I should be thanking you. You've made me into a bona fide geocacher."

Dylan glanced at the coin one more time before getting out of the car. He paused, holding the door open. "See ya." He waited another few seconds before shutting the door, and Mr. Lyman waved through the window. Dylan sighed and trudged toward his garage.

"Say, Dylan?" Mr. Lyman had rolled down the passenger side window. "I think you forgot something."

Dylan jogged back to the Prius and ducked his head so he could see through the open window. Mr. Lyman reached his arm out, holding the geocoin in his hand.

"Really? I can have it?"

Mr. Lyman nodded. "On one condition. I get to go with you when you move it to another cache."

"Deal!" Dylan took the geocoin, waved, and ran back to his house. Once inside, he didn't stop but ran all the way upstairs to the office.

"Dylan? Is that you?" his mom called from somewhere in the house.

"Yeah, it's me!" He wiggled the mouse across the mouse pad to wake up the computer and typed in the web address for the geocache homepage. In a few clicks he found the tracking site. He typed in the individual letters and numbers on the keyboard then hit "enter."

"Come on," he mumbled, waiting for the screen to pop up. When it did, an image of the wind geocoin appeared on the screen. Below it was the last known location coordinates and cache title, "Wind Beneath My Wings."

Dylan scrolled down farther and saw a web address listed in the middle of the page. He clicked it and was directed to a new web site. It was a blog page with the title "GeoTalk" across the top in bold red letters. The blog had postings about the best caches across the country, tips for finding hidden caches, and photos of the blog owner on hunts, who looked like a college student. Dylan was about to close out the page when part of a photo caught his eye. It was a building with the word "Museum" across the front. He scrolled down so he could see the entire photo. He knew that building. It was the museum in front of Dove Mountain!

He scanned the text below. It talked about EarthCaches and how Dove Mountain was listed for a short time as an EarthCache before it caved in earlier this summer. He scrolled to the bottom of the page where one comment was posted. It read, "*Hoped to find this listing now that Dove Mountain is being dug out and restored but came up empty handed. The crystal cache is missing*."

"What?" Dylan stood up, knocking the keyboard tray with his legs. His eyes focused on the last sentence: "the crystal cache is missing." The comment was about the earth crystal! He looked at the date posted next to the comment. It was from yesterday. He read it again, a wave of heat climbing up his spine. Somebody knew the earth crystal wasn't in the mine!

Dylan paced around the office. Who could possibly know the crystal was missing? Mr. Paine? Colonel Thornton? That didn't make sense. The blog comment was posted yesterday, and this morning Mr. Paine said they were still looking for it. Did someone from the construction crew know about the crystal? Or maybe someone from 4E Labs posted the comment. Somebody was trying to tell someone else about the crystal. There were so many possibilities who it might be.

He leaned over the desk and looked at the name listed beside the comment. It read "Mile High." That was the same name listed for the cache owner. Suddenly Dylan realized what he had done. The wind geocoin had been left for the person this message was meant for, but Dylan had found it first.

Thoughts fired through his brain like he was under attack. Should he just put the geocoin back in its cache? Should he tell Mr. Paine about it? Should he ask Mr. Lyman what he thought? Then he realized there was one person he needed to show this to first—Tera. She would know exactly what to do.

Dylan grabbed his phone and sent her a text.

MAJOR NEWS. CALL ME SOON AS YOU GET BACK.

EVERYTHING OK?

I FOUND SOMETHING. JUST HURRY.

BE THERE IN 30!

Dylan printed off the blog page and took it into his room along with the geocoin. How was the wind element related to all this? Was there a wind crystal after all? Dylan's mind continued to pepper him with possibilities.

After a while the doorbell rang, and he raced down the stairs to answer it.

"It's your girlfriend," Jordan sang from the living room.

Dylan opened the door and yanked Tera inside by the arm.

"This must be serious. What's going on?" she asked.

"Come up to my room, and I'll tell you."

"Leave the bedroom door open," Jordan teased.

Dylan bounded up the stairs and shut his bedroom door once Tera was in his room.

"You're freaking me out. What did you find?"

Dylan took a deep breath. "I went geocaching with Mr. Lyman this morning and we found this." He held out the geocoin. "It's the symbol for the wind element."

Tera's eyes opened wide as she took the coin.

"I typed in the tracking code and found a link for a geocache website. I spaced it off at first, but then I saw the comment posted at the bottom." He handed her the printout from the blog page and pointed out the comment.

"Right there. Read it." He watched her lips move slightly. He knew she was done when they stopped, but she didn't look up right away. "Well? What do you think?"

Tera's gaze snapped up from the paper. "I think you need to leave a comment on the blog."

"What?" Dylan backed up a few steps. "What do you mean leave a comment?"

"I mean you need to leave your own message and try to figure out who this person is."

"I thought you'd say we should show this to your dad, not try to become best friends with this guy. What if it's someone from 4E Labs?"

"There's no way I'm showing this to my dad. It's proof the crystal isn't in the mine, and we already agreed nobody can find out about that."

A sliver of guilt wiggled its way through Dylan. "Um, about that. Mr. Lyman kind of knows I switched the crystal."

Tera opened her mouth like she was about to yell.

"I didn't tell him, I swear. He figured it out. But he's not going to say anything. I totally trust him."

"How do you know Mr. Lyman didn't write that comment? Wasn't he the one who told you about the cache in the first place?"

Dylan considered it for half a second. "Why would he want me to find the message? He could have just come out and said it. No, this is definitely from someone else."

"Which is why you have to post a comment."

"What am I supposed to say? 'Who is this?'"

"Say you know where the crystal is." Tera looked serious.

"Are you crazy? It's bad enough somebody might

come looking for it, and in case you forgot, the earth crystal is right here in this room!"

Tera's face lost its color, and she looked around with wild eyes.

"It's okay. It's hidden. I'm not going to let you touch it." The room fell silent for several seconds. "So you really think I should leave a comment?"

"I do. And maybe you don't have to say you know where the crystal is. Just say you know *about* the crystal."

"Then what?"

Tera shrugged. "Then we wait and see if you get a response."

Dylan took a deep breath. "Okay." He opened his bedroom door and walked down to the office. He sat down on the black leather chair and placed his fingers on the keyboard.

Tera stood behind him. "Do you know what you're going to say?"

Dylan started typing but then hit the backspace button. He stared at the blinking curser then tried again. "*Dear Mile High, I found your wind geocoin, and I know about the crystal cache*."

"What do you think?" He swiveled his chair and faced Tera.

"I think you'll definitely get 'Mile High's' attention."

Dylan spun back around and faced the screen. He typed in a title beside the 'name' box. "*Cache is King*."

Tera chuckled. "That's a good one."

"Thanks." Dylan moved the mouse and hovered the arrow cursor above the "submit" button. "Here's goes nothin'." With a tap, he clicked the mouse and posted his message.

Chapter Nine

Dylan spun the dial until he found the first number to his locker combination. He turned it left to the next number and then right to the final one. He pulled up on the black lever and opened the red metal door with a bang. A text book wrapped in brown grocery bag paper slid off the top shelf and landed on top of his foot.

"I'm gonna kill EJ." He picked up the book and threw it back on the top shelf. Three days into the new school year and EJ's half of the locker was already a wreck. Crumpled papers were jammed in between all the text books EJ forgot to bring to class, and he asked Dylan for their locker combination every day at lunch even though it was stored in his own cell phone.

Dylan slammed his locker door and glanced down the hall. Tera and Kari were both at their locker, heads together, giggling. The inside of their locker looked like a mini version of his sister's frilly bedroom. Purple paper lined the inside and silver fringe covered the edge of the shelf. A square mirror fit on the inside of the door with a dry erase board below it. As he walked up to them, Dylan noticed a message written on it that said, "10 Days."

"What's in ten days?"

The girls whipped around. "My birthday," Kari said. "We've started the countdown. Did you get your invitation to the luau?"

"Yeah, I got it." But he wasn't about to wear a grass skirt or some ugly Hawaiian shirt like the invite suggested.

Kari grinned. "Good. And don't let EJ come up with some lame excuse why he can't come." She closed their locker door. "I gotta go. I have French class way over in the new wing, and Mademoiselle Pearlman makes you sing the French national anthem if you're late." She hurried down the hall.

"Where are you headed?" Tera asked.

"Art. You?"

"English. Hey, did you check the blog this morning?"

"Yep. Still nothing. What if 'Mile High' isn't responding because he knows I'm not the right person?"

Tera walked slowly. "I think he just hasn't checked the blog yet. I'm sure he'll respond. He'll be interested in anyone who knows about the crystal."

"I hope so. I really want to ask if he knows about any other crystals. Did Colonel Thornton give back Mr. Lyman's book?"

"Not yet. He ended up going on his fishing trip today, and he took the book with him."

Dylan stopped in front of his classroom door. "He went on his trip? I would have thought he'd have lots to do after finding…"

Tera faced Dylan. "Finding what?"

"Uh, well." He couldn't keep a secret from her. "Finding Frank."

Tera's eyes narrowed to slits.

"I wanted to tell you, but your dad said you'd get upset. Are you mad?"

Her shoulders settled. "I'm glad he's really gone.

But you should have told me."

"I know. I'm sorry. I was going to, but then all this blog stuff happened." Dylan wanted to hit his head against a locker.

Tera didn't look convinced. "I gotta go. See ya later." She walked into the classroom across the hall.

"Stupid," Dylan hissed as he went into his classroom. He had to make it up to Tera and prove she could trust him. He promised himself he'd never keep a secret from her again.

* * *

He was quiet in the car on the way home from school.

"How was your day?" his mom asked.

"Fine."

"Do you have any homework?"

"A little." Dylan checked his phone to see if Tera had responded to the text he sent right after school, apologizing again. No messages.

When he got home, he grabbed a granola bar from the kitchen pantry, a soda from the fridge, and sat down at the table to get his homework out of the way: a page of equations out of his pre-algebra book. He barely got started when his cell phone buzzed. He scrambled to pull it out of his pocket. His hopes soared when he saw it was from Tera.

HAVE U CHECKED THE BLOG?

Dylan typed quickly. NOT YET. NEED TO DO MATH FIRST.

Why was Tera so worried about the blog? He'd

checked it twice a day every day, and there hadn't been any response yet.

THERE'S A NEW COMMENT. MILE HIGH WROTE BACK.

Dylan stared at his phone for a second and then ran out of the kitchen, bounding up the stairs two at a time. He rounded the corner into the office and stopped when he saw Jordan sitting in front of the computer.

"I need to look something up really quick," he said, breathless.

His sister didn't look away from the screen. "I'm working on something."

"But I need it."

"I said I'm busy." Jordan flashed him a glare.

"Tera just texted me and asked me to look something up for her. She's waiting."

"Oh, it's for Tera? Why didn't you say so in the first place?" Jordan said in a mocking tone as she pushed her chair away from the desk.

Dylan hunched over the keyboard and typed in the blog web address. As soon as it loaded he scrolled down to the comments section. There was a reply below his post.

"*Dear Cache is King, how many crystal caches have you found?*"

Dylan read the last part over and over. *How many crystal caches have you found?* Mile High confirmed it—there was more than one crystal!

"Are you done?" Jordan asked behind him.

"Yeah. For now." Dylan ran to his room while dialing Tera's number. She answered on the first ring.

"Did you read it?" Her voice sounded excited.

"I just did. He asked how many I had!"

"Did you write back?"

"What? No. What am I supposed to say?"

Tera paused on the other end of the phone. "Tell him you have the earth crystal and ask if he has any of the others."

"Are you crazy? We don't even know who this person is."

"He doesn't know who you are either. But it's our only lead to finding the rest of the crystals."

Now it was Dylan's turn to pause. "You're not worried this person might be with 4E Labs?" He had seen enough spy movies to know it was possible to track computer internet addresses to people.

"I hope it is someone from 4E Labs."

Now Dylan was convinced she had gone crazy.

"If we play this just right, we can catch them red handed, and then my dad and Colonel Thornton can finally prove 4E Labs is behind everything." Tera's voice sounded like a plea.

"Okay." Dylan went back into the office. Jordan shook her head as soon as she saw him. Dylan mouthed "please" and his sister threw up her arms, groaned, and stormed out of the office.

"How about this?" He typed as he spoke. "*Dear Mile High, I have the earth crystal. Do you know where the others are?*"

"Perfect," Tera said. "Now we just have to wait again."

Dylan clicked the "submit" button, closed out the web page, and then remembered he wanted to print it out; he was keeping a record in case Mr. Paine needed it. He opened the blog page back up and was about to hit "print" when he noticed another comment below the one he just posted.

"Tera, Mile High replied back already. He must be online right now!"

"What does it say?"

Dylan read the comment out loud. "*Dear Cache is King, the crystals are not to be taken lightly. Many people want them, but they don't know how to use them. Do you?*"

"Hurry, write back before he goes offline," Tera said.

Dylan's fingers shook as he typed. "*Dear Mile High, I know how powerful the crystals are, which is why I want to protect them.*" He hit "send," waited a minute and then refreshed the page.

"There's a response! '*Dear Cache is King, I too want to protect the crystals, just like I protect the air we breathe*.' What does that mean?"

"Oh my gosh, it means he has the wind crystal—he protects the air—wind, air, get it?" Tera chattered.

Dylan's fingers flew over the keyboard. "*Dear Mile High, do you have the wind crystal? What does it do?*" He clicked submit and then refreshed his page a dozen times before seeing the response.

"*Dear Cache is King, I've never witnessed the wind crystal in action.*"

"That means he doesn't have the catalyst for the wind element!" Dylan's words sunk in, and he wished he could take them back.

Tera was silent for several seconds. "Tell him you have it. Tell him you have the catalyst."

"Uh-uh. No way."

"Do it, Dylan. This might be our only chance."

Dylan scowled at the monitor as he typed. "*Dear Mile High, I know how to make the crystals work. I have what they need, and it's safe.*" His pointer hovered over the "submit" button. He didn't like referring to Tera as "it." He finally clicked and sent the message. He shook his head at the screen as he refreshed it, waiting for a response.

A minute later, a new comment popped up. "Here it is! '*Dear Cache is King, we need to work together. Your crystal isn't safe, and neither is the girl.*'"

Chapter Ten

A chilling fear grabbed hold of Dylan as he read Mile High's last words again—*your crystal isn't safe and neither is the girl.* The doorbell brought him back to the present, and a minute later Tera joined Dylan in the office.

"What do we do now?" Dylan whispered the words to Tera as though Mile High could hear them through the computer.

Tera let out a breath. "Keep going."

"What do you mean?"

"I mean, keep the conversation going."

Dylan shook his head. "We can't. We need to tell your dad. Mile High knows about you. It's not safe anymore."

Tera stepped in front of Dylan and leaned over the keyboard. The keys clicked as she typed, much faster than Dylan had.

Dear Mile High, how do you know about the crystals? Are you friend or foe?

Dylan scoffed at her comment. "Friend or foe? That sounds like something out of a spy show."

"I'm cutting to the chase. We need to find out who this person is." She clicked "submit."

She hit the refresh button on the browser several times before a response was posted.

Dear Cache is King, I have been tracking the crystals for many years. I want to keep them out of the wrong hands. I am a friend.

Dylan frowned at the computer. There it was again, that phrase: “keep them out of the wrong hands.” It seemed like everyone was saying that about the crystals.

Tera started typing again. *Dear Mile High, how do we know you’re a friend and not working for the enemy?*

“Why don’t you just say 4E Labs?” Dylan asked.

“Because I don’t want to name names online.” She clicked “submit” again.

A minute later the response came back. *Dear Cache is King, I know which enemy you are referring to, and I promise I am not one of them.*”

Tera typed a two-word response. *Prove it.*

Dylan snickered. “Kinda pushy, aren’t you?”

“Hey, at least I’m getting results.” She flashed a glare toward Dylan then gave him a sheepish look. “Sorry. I didn’t mean to be that way with you.”

Dylan put his hands up in mock defense. “No problem. I’ll just stay out of your way.”

They waited several minutes with no response. Tera started chewing on her fingernail. “Maybe I was a little rude. I hope I didn’t scare him off.”

The reply finally came a few minutes later. *Dear Cache is King, I can give you a good faith offering. A way to prove I am a worthy ally. I have part of the wind crystal. The other half is located in a cache, but I’m not able to get to it. If you agree to meet with me, I will give you the coordinates. Once you find the crystal, post a comment, and I will give you instructions where to meet.*

“Do you see that? He has the wind crystal! Or part

of it. Why is it split in half?" Dylan's words rambled out of his mouth. Finally, after searching all summer, he had proof that other crystals existed.

Tera frowned. "I don't know. But I'm more interested in why Mile High can't get to the cache."

"Maybe he doesn't live here, or he's got a broken leg or something."

Instead of responding to Dylan, Tera typed a response. *Agreed. Give me the coordinates to the wind crystal, and I'll post a comment when I've found it.*

Thirty seconds after submitting it, Mile High posted a response—the coordinates for a cache.

"We did it! We know where the wind crystal is!" Dylan held up his hand for a high-five.

Tera turned toward him with her hands on her hips. "*We?*"

Dylan's face grew hot. "Okay, *you* did it. And now we get to go find the cache."

"But we don't know where it is. What if it's not even in Colorado?"

Dylan brushed past her and sat down in the office chair. He highlighted the cache coordinates with his cursor and copied it. Then he opened up a GPS web page where he pasted the coordinates into the search box. Within seconds, it listed the city and state for the location—Boulder, Colorado.

Dylan jumped out of the chair. "It's here! It's in Colorado!"

"I haven't been to Boulder. Isn't it far away?"

"It takes about an hour to get there. We go every summer to see the street performers: jugglers, magicians, and stuff. It's pretty cool."

Tera looked impressed. "We'll need someone to take us. And I'm not asking my dad. I don't want him getting involved, at least not yet. What about your sister?"

Dylan rolled his eyes. "Uh-uh. It's not worth the pain of asking her for a favor."

"You could ask Mr. Lyman."

Dylan considered the suggestion. Mr. Lyman would probably do it, but it seemed like a lot to ask. And he wasn't sure he wanted to involve Mr. Lyman with the crystals any more than he already had.

Tera's cell phone buzzed, and she checked the text. "It's Kari. She wants to know what we found out. Can I tell her?"

"Sure." Dylan figured Tera would tell her either way.

Tera's thumbs flew over the screen of her cell phone. "She's coming over. Let's meet her out front."

Dylan closed out the web pages then followed Tera downstairs and outside to his front porch. He didn't mind telling Kari about Mile High, but he knew she'd want to go on the geocache hunt with them. He and Tera had worked on this together, and he wanted just the two of them to find it together too.

Kari jogged across the street, wearing pink sweat pants with the legs pushed up and a pink and purple tie-dye T-shirt. Her white flip-flops slapped against her heels as she ran. She hopped onto the front porch. "So, tell me!"

Tera glanced at Dylan for approval. "We had a whole conversation online and found out there are other crystals."

Kari opened her mouth as if to scream. "What? No way! Where?"

"Half of the wind crystal is right here in Colorado. Mile High has the other half."

Kari turned to Dylan. "Half? That's weird. Did he say what the catalyst is?"

Dylan shook his head. "He doesn't know. But he does know that Tera is the catalyst for the earth crystal. He didn't use her name, but he did say 'the girl isn't safe.'"

Kari looked back and forth between Dylan and Tera. He knew she was thinking the same thing he was—whether or not Tera could be the catalyst for the wind crystal too. She didn't say anything though.

Tera didn't seem to notice. She sat down cross-legged in the grass beside the front walk, picking individual blades of grass and piling them in front of her. "Mile High said he couldn't get to the cache, so he asked us to do it. He wants to meet once we have it."

Kari's mouth dropped open again. "Meet? With him? But you don't even know who it is! What if it's somebody from 4E Labs? What if he tries taking..." Her gaze drifted to Tera and back.

"That won't happen," Dylan snapped.

Kari frowned. "What's your plan? Find half of the wind crystal and then what? If you meet with Mile High, he's going to want you to give it to him."

Dylan sat on the top porch step and ran his hands through his hair. "I don't know yet. I need to find the wind crystal first. I'll figure out the rest from there." He wasn't going to tell the girls, but he did have a plan. He knew he couldn't involve Mr. Paine, but there was someone just as knowledgeable about the crystals—Colonel Thornton. He'd be able to help when it was time for Dylan to meet

Mile High, and if it turned out to be someone from 4E Labs, then the colonel would be there to catch him. Tera wouldn't have to be involved, and Dylan wouldn't have to break his promise about keeping their secret.

"So exactly where is the cache?" Kari asked.

Tera held up her pile of grass and let it blow away in the breeze. "It's in Boulder. We have the coordinates. All we need now is to figure out a way to get there. Somebody needs to drive us, but we don't agree on who." She smirked at Dylan.

"I know how we can get there." A grin spread across Kari's face. "In fact, I have the perfect plan."

Dylan had to stop himself from groaning. Kari was going to take over the entire thing and try to boss everyone around, just like she always did.

"What's the plan?" Tera jumped up off the ground.

"I have a soccer tournament in Boulder this Saturday. You guys can come along, I know my parents won't mind. I usually play a bunch of games throughout the day, but in between we can go look for the cache."

"That is the perfect the plan! What do you think, Dylan?"

He looked at his friends. He had to admit, it solved their problem of getting up to Boulder. And as long as he got his hands on the wind crystal, he really didn't care how he did it, or who came along with him.

"I think we're going geocaching this weekend."

Chapter Eleven

"Goooo Kari!" Tera clapped and cheered from the sidelines. Kari's soccer team was winning by two goals with only five minutes left in the first game of the morning. Dylan sat in a red fold-out chair beside Tera. He pulled down on the brim of the faded Colorado Rockies baseball hat EJ had given him last spring. Too bad EJ had football and couldn't come to Boulder with them. It would have been nice not to be the only boy there. But EJ probably would have made fun of the girls, even though they looked tougher than half the middle school football players.

Dylan took out his GPS and brought up the screen with the coordinates for the wind crystal. According to the device, it wasn't far from the soccer field. He had assumed it would be located somewhere near the foothills, but this looked like it was in the middle of town, near a bunch of stores. Hopefully that meant it'd be easy to get to, and Kari's mom wouldn't mind taking them as soon as the game was over.

Cheers erupted around him, and Tera jumped out of her chair, wooting with the crowd.

"Did you see that? Kari just scored!" Tera's pony tail swung back and forth as she bounced on her toes.

"Does that mean the game's over?" Dylan adjusted his hat and noticed the two teams walking in opposite lines giving each other high-fives. He stood up and folded his chair.

Kari ran up to them, her face flush and her curly hair wet with sweat. Her mom gave her a hug and handed her a sports drink.

"You were amazing!" Tera picked up Kari's bag off the ground.

"Yeah, good game." Dylan picked up Mrs. Johansen's folding chair and stuffed it in its bag.

"Thanks. Our next game is at three, so we have plenty of time to look for the cache and still get some lunch." Kari drained half the bottle and let out a loud sigh. "Do you know where to go?"

Dylan nodded and followed the girls across the field to the parking lot. He loaded the chairs into the back of Mrs. Johansen's minivan and climbed in the open sliding door. "We need to get to Broadway."

Mrs. Johansen looked at him in the rearview mirror. "And this is for some sort of geology project?"

Dylan gave Kari a confused look.

"It's a geocache, Mom. And it's more of a hobby than a project." Kari shook her head.

Dylan gave Mrs. Johansen the rest of the directions from the GPS. "It should be somewhere on the next block." But as he looked out the windows of the minivan and noticed a drycleaners, gas station, and a sandwich shop, he started to wonder whether Mile High had told the truth. This didn't look like someplace where a cache would be hidden.

"You have arrived at your destination," the GPS announced.

"Does that mean I should stop?" Mrs. Johansen

stepped a little too hard on the break, causing the minivan to lurch forward.

A used car lot was on the left side of the street, and an old light-colored, one-story brick building was on the right. A black and yellow sign across the store front said "Pawn Shop."

"What do we do now?" Tera asked.

Dylan unbuckled his seatbelt. "Let's look around."

Mrs. Johansen pulled into the parking lot of the pawn shop and followed the kids out of the car. "Are you sure this is where you wanted to go?" She clutched her purse against her chest.

Dylan turned in a slow circle. Without a cache title or any hints, he had no idea where to look. He scanned the front of the pawn shop again. Neon-colored poster boards hung in the windows that said "20% Off All Items," "Engagement Rings," and "Pawn or Sell." Then he noticed a smaller sign taped to the glass door. It read "Gems and Precious Stones." The sign had a drawing of a diamond in a triangle shape. It gave him an idea. It might be a long shot, but it was all he had to go on.

"Let's go in the pawn shop." He jogged toward the door.

"I don't think that's a good idea," Mrs. Johansen called after him.

"It's fine, Mom. Come on." Kari and Tera hurried toward the shop while Dylan held the door open for them.

The inside of the store was a cramped square room filled with small glass cases that held guns, watches, and jewelry. Lawn mowers and power tools lined the back wall. Framed posters and memorabilia hung all around the store, and tables piled with boxes of books, records, and other junk were scattered down the middle. The place smelled like fast food bags that had been left in a car too long.

Dylan wandered through the store, peering into the glass cases. Tera and Kari looked through a stack of books while Mrs. Johansen hovered not more than a few inches away from them.

"Hey kids, there's no loitering in here." The gruff voice came from a hefty man wearing a faded black T-shirt. He had stringy dark hair, tattoos on his arms and neck, and a black circle in his ear lobe.

"We're looking for something." Dylan approached the far end of the counter. "Your sign in the door says you have gems. Could I see them?"

The man put his hands on top of the counter and leaned forward. "What kind did you have in mind?"

Dylan's stomach churned as the guy's rank breath invaded his nose. "I'm looking for a clear crystal that has a triangle shape in the middle. Or in this case, half a triangle."

The man made a sucking sound, like he was trying to get a piece of food out of his teeth with his tongue. "That's pretty specific." He looked past Dylan at the girls and Mrs. Johansen, who had walked up to the counter, and then he turned his attention back to Dylan. "Let me see if I have anything that matches that description." He disappeared through a black curtain behind him.

"Why would the crystal be in a pawn shop?" Kari hissed. "I thought it was supposed to be in a cache?"

Dylan turned around and leaned his back against the counter. "Mile High never said it was in a cache. He just gave us coordinates. Maybe he thought it was safer.

Nobody would ever think to look here."

"I really think we should go." Mrs. Johansen gave them all a stern "mom" look.

Tera faced Kari and her mom. "Let's just wait and see if the guy comes back with--"

The pawn shop man appeared through the curtain. He placed a small white box on top of the counter. "The person who pawned this said to only give it to someone who could describe exactly what it looks like. So, what does the triangle look like?"

Dylan straightened his shoulders. "It's a triangle pointing up, with a line through the middle."

"Hmph." The man lifted the lid off the box. He reached in and pulled out a long gold chain. At the end dangled a pendant.

Dylan cupped the pendant in his hand. It was a clear crystal the size of a large marble, but egg shaped. The back side was flat, like it had been cut off, and in the center were several golden-colored lines at different angles—lines that if the back half of the crystal was complete, they would form an upright triangle with a line through the middle.

"This is it. The wind crystal." It was like finding the greatest treasure in the world. "We'll take it."

"Whoa." The man snatched up the pendant in his meaty fingers. "That's not how we operate here. This is gonna cost you."

Dylan looked into the tired man's eyes. "We have to pay for it?" Mile High hadn't said anything about that.

"That's the idea. And I only accept cash." The man looked right at Mrs. Johansen.

Dylan turned around. "I didn't bring any money. I

thought we were looking for a geocache."

Tera patted her shorts pockets. "All I have is a ten."

"Mom, do you have any money? We'll pay you back, I promise."

Mrs. Johansen sighed and then addressed the pawn shop employee. "How much is the necklace?"

"Two hundred."

"*Dollars?*" Dylan yelled.

"That's absurd." Mrs. Johansen stepped forward. "You expect kids to pay two hundred dollars?"

"Look lady. I don't care who pays it, as long as I get cash."

Mrs. Johansen leaned toward the man so her face was inches from his. "Well, I'm not paying. Kids, it's time to go."

Dylan's frustration turned to panic. He was so close to getting the crystal. He couldn't just walk away. "Please, can't we work out some sort of deal?"

The man folded his arms in front of his chest and peered down. "Do you have anything you can pawn?"

Dylan did a mental check. He didn't have anything of value on him. Not even his water-resistant digital watch.

"I have something to pawn." Tera stepped up to the counter. "These." She flicked her earlobes with her index fingers, showing off the diamond earrings her dad had given her for her birthday last April.

Dylan gasped. "What are you doing? You can't sell those."

"I'm not selling them. I'm pawning them. We can come back when we have the two hundred dollars and get them back."

“Tera, I don’t think that’s a good idea.” Mrs. Johansen’s voice was softer now.

“It’s okay. This is important. And I know I’ll get my earrings back.” Tera glared at the man.

He looked at each of Tera’s ears. “I’d be willing to do that. But I need an adult to sign the contract.”

“Please, Mom,” Kari begged.

It took Mrs. Johansen almost a full minute to answer. “Fine. But make sure you tell your dad about this. And you,” she got back in the man’s face, “you better be legitimate or I’ll bring you up with the Better Business Bureau.”

The man held up his hands as if to surrender. “You’ve got yourself a deal lady. I’ll get the paperwork ready.” He dropped the crystal back into the box. After Tera removed her earrings and laid them on the counter, the man slid the box toward Dylan. “I hope it’s worth it, kid.”

Dylan grinned. “It totally is.”

Chapter Twelve

Dylan held the box with the wind crystal in his lap the entire drive back from Boulder. While Kari and Tera talked about Kari's second big win of the day, his thoughts wandered to what would happen once he told Mile High that he had the other half of the crystal. Would Mile High keep his end of the bargain? Or was it all a trick to get the crystal and Tera…again? He hadn't taken the crystal back out of the box, even though he couldn't help but wonder what might happen if Tera touched it.

Mrs. Johansen turned onto their street and pulled into her driveway. She hit the button to open the van door.

"Thanks again, Mrs. Johansen. Good game, Kari." Dylan climbed out and waited for Tera.

"Thanks. I'm glad it worked out. Let me know how everything goes." Kari waved as Tera got out of the van.

Dylan and Tera walked across the street and stopped in Tera's driveway.

"Can I see it?" Tera nodded toward the box in Dylan's hand. "I didn't get a very good look at it in the store."

"Are you sure?" Dylan didn't think she'd want to be anywhere near it, but maybe she was just as curious about whether or not she could be its catalyst.

Tera nodded again, and Dylan removed the box

lid, secured it on the bottom of the box, and pulled out the necklace. He held it by the chain, letting the crystal pendant dangle. It swayed back and forth, the sunlight reflecting off the bright yellow lines in the center.

"It's different than the earth crystal." Tera stepped toward it but hugged her arms to her body.

"Yeah, I know. It's smaller, but that's because it's missing half."

Tera shook her head. "No, there's something else. I don't…feel anything."

Dylan glanced at her. "What do you mean?"

"It's hard to explain. But when I'm around the earth crystal, I get a strange feeling. There's this slight pull I have, like a magnet, and even the hair on my arms point to it. I don't feel that with this one."

Dylan piled the necklace in his hand and held it out in front of her. "Here. Take it."

Tera stumbled backward. "No way. I'm not touching it."

"But you just said you don't have the feeling, so it's fine." Dylan shoved his hand forward.

Tera put her hands up in defense. "I'm still not risking it."

"Come on. Just take it, that way we'll know for sure."

"I said no. Why are you being so pushy?" Tera glowered at him.

Dylan's desperation took over. He had to know if she was the catalyst for the wind crystal. "If you can't activate it, then we don't have to worry about 4E Labs coming after you again, at least not for this. You'd finally be safe."

"Safe? *Safe?* As long as 4E Labs is out there, I'll never be safe. And I don't need you testing the crystal on me. Is that the only reason why you wanted me to come with you today? To see if I was a catalyst?"

"No! That had nothing to do with it. I only brought it up because you just said…never mind." Dylan dropped the crystal back into the box and jammed the lid on. "I just thought it'd be helpful if we knew," he mumbled.

"Why are you so determined to find all four crystals? It's like you're obsessed." Tera's words stung like a stray spark from a campfire.

"I'm not obsessed. You of all people know what the crystals can do and what 4E Labs is capable of. Somebody has to stop them. And if you'd just let me tell your dad the truth then I wouldn't have to do all this. He could be in charge."

"So this is *my* fault?"

"I didn't say that." Dylan hated it when people twisted his words.

"You didn't have to. I know it's what you meant." Tera's eyes looked a darker shade of green. "Sometimes I wish I'd never moved here. I could go back to California and live with my grandparents. At least I'd be far away from 4E Labs and far away from…" Tera stopped.

Dylan's heart stopped too. "Far away from me?"

"I was going to say far away from the earth crystal."

This time her words didn't sound so harsh, but Dylan had already been wounded.

Tera let her arms drop to her sides. "I think you should give the wind crystal to Mile High, and then be done with this whole thing."

"But we don't know who Mile High is!"

"I don't care. I want this to stop. Please, Dylan. Promise me you'll hand over the necklace, and then end it."

Dylan stared at the small white box in his hand. The words "I promise" sat on his tongue like a giant sour gumball, but he couldn't spit them out. He knew he couldn't keep the promise.

Tera snatched the box out of his hand.

"What are you doing?"

"I'll hold the crystal, and if I'm not the catalyst, then will you promise to give all this up?"

"You don't have to do that." Even as he said the words, Dylan didn't believe them.

Tera removed the lid and pulled the necklace out by its chain. Then she wrapped her right hand around the crystal. After several seconds she let go, leaving the necklace dangling.

Dylan watched the crystal, looking for the slightest glow from the yellow triangle in the middle. Nothing. "I didn't see it flash or anything, did you?" He glanced at Tera.

She let out a slow breath and shook her head. "I guess I'm not the catalyst."

Dylan's initial relief was quickly replaced by concern. If she wasn't the catalyst for the wind crystal, then who was?

"I guess it'll be Mile High's problem now," Tera said. She eyed Dylan. "You're going to keep your promise, right?"

"Yeah, I'm going to keep it. I'll contact Mile High right now and tell him I have the other half of the wind crystal."

Tera put the necklace back into the box and handed it to Dylan. "Are you going to meet him in person?"

"No, I think I'll set up a new geocache instead and give Mile High the coordinates."

"It'd be nice to know who Mile High is though."

Tera's comment gave Dylan an idea. "What if I set up a trail cam? I've seen geocachers talk about them on the website."

"A trail cam? That sounds expensive."

Dylan shrugged. "I don't think they're more than a hundred bucks. I have money saved up. I could set up the cam when I leave the cache. Once we know who Mile High is, we could give the video to your dad and Colonel Thornton."

Tera seemed to consider the suggestion. "That could work. Maybe my dad and the colonel will forget about the earth crystal if they have the wind crystal and Mile High to worry about."

Dylan noticed the hope in Tera's voice. "So you're okay with it?"

"Yeah. I think it's a good plan. Where are you going to put the cache?"

Dylan hadn't had a chance to think about that yet. "I don't know. The easiest place would be in the creek behind my house."

Tera shook her head. "That's too close. If Mile High is someone from 4E Labs, they'd know right away one of us was Cache is King. It needs to be farther away."

"I could put it back at Chatfield State Park. We know Mile High is able to get there."

"But then you have to get someone to take you again."

"Maybe Mr. Lyman would do it. He seemed to really like geocaching when we went the other day. I'll ask him."

Tera looked satisfied. "Okay. I better get home. Let me know what Mile High says." She fidgeted with her fingers. "Thanks."

"For what?" Dylan asked.

"For making me find out if I was a catalyst. I'm really glad I finally know."

Dylan kicked at a chunk of grass in the yard. "Me too. And I'm glad you don't have to worry about it." He couldn't help smiling in relief.

Tera gave a little wave and walked inside. Dylan jogged across the street to his house. Once inside, he headed straight upstairs. His mom was in her bedroom folding laundry.

"I'm back," he said as he passed her door.

"How was the soccer game?" Mrs. Fisher yelled down the hall.

"Good!" Dylan sat down at the computer and pulled up the GeoTalk blog. He scrolled down to the last comment Mile High had left and typed a comment. "*I have the crystal but not the catalyst. I'll return it to the wind beneath my wings cache tomorrow.*" He clicked the submit button and went down the hall to his bedroom. He dug his red nylon wallet out of his dresser drawer and pulled out the wad of cash. He counted out a hundred dollars—money he had saved up over the years from birthdays, allowance, and extra chores. He tried not to spend it in case he needed it for something really important, and this was definitely important. He folded up the bills and stuck them in his pocket. Then he went down to his mom's bedroom.

"Mom, can you take me to the sporting goods store? I need to buy a trail camera for geocaching. I have my own money and everything."

His mom glanced at him over a large bath towel. "I suppose. If that's what you want to spend your money on."

"I do. And I want to ask Mr. Lyman to take me geocaching again at Chatfield State Park. I need to place a cache there." Dylan took two of his socks out of the laundry basket and folded them together.

"I'm sure he'd enjoy that. He mentioned several times at dinner the other night what a good time he had geocaching. He actually said it was like a breath of fresh air."

Dylan stopped folding. "He said that?" Suddenly he thought back to all the comments from Mile High. What if Mile High was Mr. Lyman? It made sense. He had the book on the crystals, and he knew right where to go at Chatfield State Park. But then why make Dylan go to the pawn shop? Couldn't he go himself? And was there a connection to Mr. Lyman and 4E Labs, or was Mr. Lyman truly trying to protect the crystals from them? If Mr. Lyman was Mile High, Dylan would find out soon enough.

Chapter Thirteen

Dylan tested the trail cam one more time while he waited for Mr. Lyman to pick him up. He turned the unit on, walked back and forth in front of it a few times, and then turned it back off, satisfied it would work. The camouflage design on the device was a nice touch. He was convinced he could hide it underneath the trash can with the cache, and Mile High would never see it.

The doorbell rang, and he slipped the trail cam into his backpack. He answered the door, surprised to find Kari instead of Mr. Lyman standing on the front porch.

"Oh good, you're home. Tera and EJ are both gone, and I need someone to help me with my social studies project."

Dylan gave a quick laugh. "You need help with homework? That's a first."

Kari smirked. "I just need you to answer my survey on recycling habits. It's only eight questions and won't take long." She shoved a sheet of paper toward Dylan.

"Can't. Sorry. I'm waiting for Mr. Lyman to pick me up so we can go back to Chatfield State Park and leave the wind crystal cache."

Kari's face brightened. "Can I come? I won't make you fill out my survey if you let me go with you."

Dylan snickered, surprised she'd give up so easily on the survey to go geocaching. "Deal."

"Thanks. But don't tell EJ and Tera you got out of taking the survey. I still need both of them to fill it out. Let me run home and tell my mom I'm going with you. I'll be right back." Kari sprinted through Dylan's yard and across the street to her house.

Dylan turned to go back inside when Mr. Lyman's Prius came into view and slowly pulled into the driveway. Dylan opened the storm door and yelled to his mom, "I'm leaving! Be back later!" He didn't wait for a reply but instead walked up to the car and opened the passenger door.

Mr. Lyman greeted him with a friendly smile. "All set?"

"Yeah. Kari's coming too, if that's okay."

"The more the merrier!" Mr. Lyman reached into the back seat and shoved a pile of books to one side.

Dylan threw his backpack onto the floor of the front seat and glanced across the street toward Kari's house. He didn't want to keep Mr. Lyman waiting and breathed a sigh of relief when he saw her bound out her front door.

Kari jogged across the street carrying a water bottle in one hand and a small nylon pack over her shoulder. "Thanks for waiting." She opened the door and climbed into the back seat. "Hi, Mr. Lyman."

"Glad you could join us, Kari. Everyone set?"

Dylan buckled his seat belt and adjusted his backpack between his feet.

Mr. Lyman backed out of the driveway and headed out of the neighborhood. "You're returning the cache you found last time to the same spot, is that correct?"

Dylan glanced sideways at him. "Yep."

"Does the cache owner want the geocoin back?"

"No, it's not that. I, uh, forgot to leave something in its place. You know, only take a trackable if you leave something of equal value." Dylan didn't want to tell Mr. Lyman about the wind crystal in case he turned out to be Mile High. He wanted to catch him on camera so he had proof instead.

Kari's silence in the back seat told Dylan she was probably thinking the same thing. He knew Tera had filled her in and made her promise not to tell anyone.

During the drive, Mr. Lyman asked about school, and Kari launched into details about her soccer season. Dylan stared out the side window, watching billowing clouds race across the sky and gather in dark clumps. The small Prius drifted slightly to the right as wind gusts blew against the car from the left.

Mr. Lyman gripped the top of the steering wheel with both hands. "A pretty good wind has picked up. I wonder if a storm is moving through. I don't recall the news forecasting any rain though." He looked up through the windshield toward the sky.

Dylan glanced in the same direction. "Hopefully we can get the geocache in place before the storm hits." He didn't want anything to get in the way of putting the cache back.

They pulled into the entrance of Chatfield State Park, and Mr. Lyman drove to the same parking lot as last time. When Dylan opened his car door and got out, a blast of wind blew it clear open, and he thought the entire door was going to fly off its hinge. He struggled to close it and had to lean on it with his entire body.

As they walked across the parking lot toward the model airplane runway, the wind gusts came in spurts with periods of calm in between. When they reached the runway, it was empty, and the orange flag beside it flapped furiously against the wind.

Dylan spotted the trash can and picked up his pace. "This will only take a sec." He jogged over to the metal container, slipped his backpack off his shoulders, and knelt down behind the trash can.

Kari followed and knelt down beside him. "Are you sure your plan is going to work?"

"We'll find out." Dylan peered around the trash can. Mr. Lyman stood in the middle of the runway, his hands in the pockets of his loose brown pants, staring up at the sky. "Here, hold this." He handed Kari the box with the wind crystal and took the trail cam out of his backpack. He turned the black switch to "on" and propped it up against one of the legs of the metal container surrounding the trash can. It was hidden just enough that it wasn't noticeable, but the round camera lens would record anyone who bent down to reach under to collect the cache.

Kari removed the lid from the box and gazed at the crystal necklace in the bottom. "I'm surprised you're not keeping it. You spent all summer searching for another crystal, and when you find one, you just give it up."

Dylan sat back on his heels. "It's no good just having half, and it's more important to find out who Mile High is. Plus, Tera's not a catalyst, so she's safe with this one." He held out his hand for the box.

Kari put the lid back on and handed it to him. "What if Tera didn't activate it because it was only half? What if you need the whole thing in order to have it activated?"

Dylan thought about it for a second. "I think

something would have happened if she was the catalyst." He got on his hands and knees and reached as far as he could underneath the trash can with the box. He looked at the trail cam, satisfied that whoever came for the cache would wind up giving him a clear view of their face.

"How's it going over here?" Mr. Lyman asked from the other side of the trash can.

Dylan stood up quickly and brushed the grass off his knees. "Good. I think we're all set." He gave Kari a slight nod. She picked his backpack up and handed it to him.

Mr. Lyman walked around to their side of the trash can. "What did you leave in place of the geocoin?"

"Oh, just a rock. It's kind of my thing, leaving rocks in caches." Dylan heaved his backpack onto his shoulders and avoided Mr. Lyman's eyes. Even though it was technically the truth, somehow it still felt a little bit like lying.

Mr. Lyman smiled. "I like that, using rocks as your calling card. Only a true geologist would think of that."

Another gust of wind rushed across the runway, and Dylan grabbed onto the trash can to keep his balance.

"I think the storm's getting closer." Kari's voice carried off with the wind.

"We better go." Mr. Lyman waved them forward. Dylan and Kari hurried back across the runway.

Dylan kept his head down as he fought against the strong wind. When he reached Mr. Lyman's car, he tried opening the door carefully, but the wind blew it open. He threw his backpack on the floor of the front seat and ducked inside. Then he used both hands to pull the door closed. Mr. Lyman and Kari climbed in, and when all the doors were closed, a second of calm filled the tiny car.

"Don't worry, kids. I'll get us home safely." Mr. Lyman pushed the engine button and slowly pulled out of the parking lot. Tumbleweeds, stray pieces of litter, and green leaves blew across the road. Mr. Lyman drove slowly, hunched forward on the edge of his seat.

Even though the clouds were coated in dark grey, not a drop of rain had fallen. They passed only a few cars on the winding road toward home. With each gust of wind, Dylan's stomach jumped, afraid the car would be shoved off the road. But the closer they got to their neighborhood, the more Dylan relaxed in his seat.

"I hope we don't get a downpour tonight," Kari said. "Then the soccer fields will be flooded for my game tomorrow."

Dylan looked at her over his shoulder. She gnawed on her fingernails like a hamster eating sunflower seeds. He turned back around and something on the side of the road caught his eye. A swirling mass of dust about the same size as the Prius drifted toward them. Before he could say anything, the tiny tornado bumped into his side of the car, sending it spinning.

Mr. Lyman slammed on the breaks. Kari screamed, and Dylan saw nothing but sky, clouds, and trees pass before his eyes. He felt the car go over a large bump and suddenly they were upside down. In the next second they were right side up, then tumbled upside down again. He covered his head with his arms and closed his eyes as the car slid along its roof for what felt like forever. It finally came to a sudden stop like the end of a terrifying roller coaster ride.

"Are you guys okay?" Kari's voice trembled.

Dylan tried twisting in his seat to look at her, but his seatbelt was stretched tight across his chest. "I think so. You?"

"Yeah. Is Mr. Lyman all right?"

Dylan wiggled in his seat until he could see Mr. Lyman who was slumped forward with his head resting on the steering wheel. "Mr. Lyman?" He reached out and shook his shoulder. That's when he noticed blood trickling down Mr. Lyman's face.

Chapter Fourteen

"Mr. Lyman! Mr. Lyman are you okay?" Dylan shook his neighbor's shoulder. A low moan answered him. "He's alive, but he's bleeding pretty bad. We need to get help." Dylan reached for his seatbelt release button. As soon as he clicked it, he realized his mistake, but it was too late. He banged his head on the ceiling of the upside down car as the seatbelt that had kept him in place gave way. He fumbled for the door and managed to get it open, then climbed out into the dry grassy ditch beside the road.

The sight of the dented Prius startled him. A spider-web crack filled the middle of the windshield, and bits of red glass from a broken brake light were scattered in the dirt. With its black tires exposed in the air, the car looked like a bug stuck on its back.

Dylan ran to Kari's side. Her door had opened during the crash and its window shattered. He reached in to help her out. "Are you okay?"

Kari nodded, but her face was pale and her eyes looked dazed. She opened Mr. Lyman's door and leaned in. "Can you get my phone?" she said over her shoulder. "We need to call 9-1-1. I think it's in the back seat somewhere."

Dylan crawled into the back seat and spotted a pink

phone case lying on the car's ceiling. He grabbed it. Luckily, it hadn't broken. He pushed the emergency dial button.

"Nine-one-one, what's your emergency?" said a voice on the other end.

"Uh, yeah, we've been in a car accident, and my neighbor is hurt."

"What is your location?"

Dylan looked around for a sign, but he couldn't see up the hill they had rolled down. "We're on the back road that leads from Castle Pines to Chatfield State Park. A dust devil made our car roll into a ditch."

"Stay on the line. Help is on the way."

Dylan crawled backwards out of the car and stood beside Kari who was still kneeling beside Mr. Lyman. She spoke softly to him, her hand resting on his back. "An ambulance should be here soon," Dylan said. Kari just nodded again.

Dylan's muscles tingled as irritation built up. Standing there was useless, but he couldn't do anything to help Mr. Lyman. He handed the phone to Kari. "Here. We're supposed to stay on the line until the ambulance shows up. I'm going to go stand by the side of the road. They might not see us down in this ditch." Kari nodded and took the phone. Dylan walked around the front of the car and made his way up the steep embankment. A rush of air from a truck barreling by forced him to keep his distance from the road. A second earlier and he could have waved down the trucker for help. He looked in both directions, but no other cars were coming. The wind had died down and most of the clouds had moved out toward the mountains.

He paced along the road's shoulder, glancing down at the Prius every few minutes. He wished he hadn't asked Mr. Lyman to take him geocaching. Then he wouldn't be hurt, lying upside down in a ditch. He should just have shown him the wind crystal and asked if he was Mile High. He shouldn't have tried to be sneaky. If Mr. Lyman ended up being okay, Dylan was going to tell him everything.

Dylan realized his parents didn't know what had happened. He remembered his cell phone was in his shorts pocket, so he fished it out and dialed his home number.

"Hello?" Of course Jordan was the first to answer.

"It's me. Is Mom home?"

"Nope. Mom and Dad ran to the store. What do you need?"

A lump inched its way from Dylan's chest into his throat. He didn't know if he could say the next words without it turning into a sob. "We were in a car accident. Mr. Lyman is hurt, and the paramedics are coming." He closed his eyes tight to fight back the tears.

"Oh my gosh. Are you okay? Where are you? I'll come get you."

"We're on that back road that leads to Chatfield State Park." Dylan sniffled and sucked in a big gulp of air, relieved to know his sister was coming to get him.

"I'll be right there. And I'll call Mom on her cell too."

Dylan hung up and wiped his nose with the bottom of his T-shirt. He sat down on the sandy dirt and hung his head between his knees. This didn't seem real.

The faint sound of a siren echoed through the

foothills. Dylan stood, straining his ears to determine which direction it was coming from. He finally saw flashing lights to the right. As soon as the red and white ambulance came into view, Dylan frantically waved his arms above his head.

The ambulance pulled onto the shoulder with an abrupt stop. The sirens turned off, but the lights continued to flash in silence. A man and a woman in navy shirts and pants hurried out of the front and approached Dylan.

"What happened?" asked the woman.

"A dust devil hit our car, and we rolled into the ditch. My neighbor, Mr. Lyman, was driving, and he's hurt." Dylan led the paramedics down the hill to the car. They brought a stretcher with them. "We haven't moved him, but he's bleeding. You need to help him."

Kari stood up and moved out of the woman's way. The paramedic leaned in to check Mr. Lyman.

Dylan waited beside Kari, hugging his arms against his chest. The paramedic took Mr. Lyman's pulse and shined a small light in both his eyes.

"The cut above his eye is superficial. He may have a few broken ribs, and it appears he has a concussion. We'll take him to the hospital." The paramedic turned and faced Dylan and Kari. "Is someone on the way for you two?"

"Yeah, my sister's coming. Is Mr. Lyman going to be okay?"

"He should be." The woman gave them a slight smile. "I want to make sure you're both okay too. We'll do a quick exam once we get your neighbor secured in the ambulance." Her partner crawled into the passenger's side, carefully released the seatbelt so Mr. Lyman wouldn't fall, and helped ease him out of the car and carry him to the stretcher.

Dylan and Kari grabbed their backpacks out of the car. They followed the paramedics up the hill and watched them lift Mr. Lyman into the back of the ambulance. The man got in with him and the woman approached Kari with a stethoscope.

"Let me just take a quick listen," the woman said.

While Dylan waited for his turn a police car pulled up and parked in front of the ambulance. A broad-shouldered man with dark reflective sunglasses hurried over to them. "Rollover accident?"

The woman nodded. "The driver was injured, and we're transporting him to the Littleton Hospital. The kids seem to be okay. They're waiting to be picked up."

"You go ahead. I'll stay with them." The police officer joined Dylan and Kari on the side of the road. After the woman listened to Dylan's heart and checked his eyes, she climbed into the driver's seat. The sirens started up as the ambulance pulled out onto the street.

The police officer walked to the edge of the hill and peered down at the overturned Prius. "Can you tell me what happened?"

"A dust devil." Kari shook her head. "It came out of nowhere."

"Yeah. It looked like the Tasmanian Devil cartoon when he does that spinning thing. It started on the side of the road and spun right into us. It was like a mini tornado rammed into the side of the car and pushed us across. Then we rolled down the hill." Dylan shivered remembering the whole thing.

The police officer scribbled in a small spiral notepad.

"I'll arrange for a tow truck. You kids were lucky. It could have been a lot worse." He flipped his notepad closed and adjusted his wide-brimmed hat as he glanced at the road. "It's not safe to stand here. Let's wait in the cruiser for your ride." He held open the back door while Dylan and Kari climbed in, then he got into the driver's side and reached for his radio.

Dylan had never been in the back of a police car before. A clear window separated the front from the back and a long rifle sat upright on the other side of it. He wondered how many bad guys had sat in this very same spot.

The police officer opened a small door in the divider. "When I got the call about the accident over the radio, dispatch said the rollover involved kids, but it looks like you two are a little old for these." He held up a folded blue blanket and a small brown teddy bear.

"Yeah." Dylan gave a little laugh, but part of him wouldn't have minded holding on to that teddy bear. Instead, he checked his cell phone to see if Jordan or his mom had called. "Did you call your parents?" he asked Kari.

"Yep. I told them we're fine and your sister was on her way. I texted Tera too."

Dylan hadn't thought of that. He had been too worried about Mr. Lyman. He'd call her and EJ when he got home. He glanced back at Kari. She had her eyes closed and rubbed her temples.

"Are you sure you're okay?"

Kari stopped rubbing her head but didn't open her eyes. "Yeah, I just feel kind of shaky. From the accident." She opened her eyes and looked at Dylan. "Do you think the wind storm and dust devil had something to do with the crystal?" She kept her voice to a whisper and glanced at the divider to make sure the police officer wasn't listening.

Heat rushed to Dylan's face. "Well, I do now! How could I miss that? But we don't have the catalyst. The crystal was never activated."

"What if Tera really is the catalyst? What if she activated it just enough to cause all that wind, but she needs the whole crystal to activate it even more?"

Dylan dropped his head in his hands. "I'm so stupid! How could I let her get near another crystal?" The sound of a loud car engine interrupted his thoughts. Dylan turned around, looking out the police car's rear window. He recognized his sister's red two-door coupe. The police officer got out and let Dylan and Kari out of the car. Tension melted off Dylan as his sister got out of the car and ran up to him.

"Are you guys okay?" Jordan held Dylan by the shoulders and looked him up and down. He nodded.

"Are you a relative?" the police officer asked.

"I'm his sister. Jordan Fisher. I can take them both home." She turned back to Dylan. "Mom and Dad are really worried. They wanted to pick you up but they were in Castle Rock and I was closer, so I told them we'd meet them at home."

The police officer nodded. "I'll wait for the tow truck. You kids take care."

"Thanks for your help." Dylan shook the police officer's hand. Then he and Kari hurried to Jordan's car. He held the front seat forward while Kari climbed behind it into the back. They gave Jordan a quick recap of what had happened then were silent the rest of the way home.

Jordan dropped Kari off in her driveway. “I’ll call you later.” Kari squeezed Dylan’s arm as she climbed out from the back seat.

Jordan drove them across the street to their house. Their parents’ car was in the garage when Jordan pulled in, and Dylan took a deep breath, preparing to tell the story all over again.

His mom wrapped him up in a hug before he had time to take his shoes off by the back door. “I’m so glad you’re okay.” She held him for several seconds before stepping back and holding him by the shoulders, just like Jordan had done. “I talked to the nurse at the hospital, and Mr. Lyman is stabilized and alert. I thought we could go visit him after dinner.”

Dylan nodded. He didn’t know how his mom already knew which hospital Mr. Lyman was at, but he was glad he didn’t have to talk about it.

He headed upstairs and found himself in the office. The GeoTalk blog was still pulled up on the computer. He sat down and typed a quick message to Mile High.

The wind crystal is waiting for you.

Chapter Fifteen

Dylan followed his mom down the hospital's long carpeted hallway. He hugged a stack of National Geographic magazines to his chest. He had gathered them for Mr. Lyman to read. Dylan peered into the rooms with open doors as they passed. TVs blared in some, and others had visitors surrounding the ends of hospital beds. The smell of cooked chicken filled the hall, and he noticed dinner trays piled on carts against the wall. A woman wearing dark red scrubs smiled at them from the nurse's station.

His mom stopped in front of room 325. The door was ajar, and she knocked before pushing it open. "Mr. Lyman? It's Debra and Dylan."

"Come in." Mr. Lyman's voice sounded hoarse.

Dylan and his mom stepped into the room. Mrs. Fisher walked up to the far side of the bed and kissed Mr. Lyman on top of his head. "How are you feeling?"

Mr. Lyman tried pushing himself up but winced. "Slight headache from the bump on the head, and the cracked ribs are sore, but nothing that time won't heal." He smiled and turned his attention to Dylan. "I sure am glad you and Kari are all right. I'm so sorry about what happened. I feel terrible you kids were involved."

Dylan didn't want Mr. Lyman to feel guilty. It

wasn't his fault. "We're fine. The Prius didn't look too good though. The police had it towed."

"Insurance will cover it. I'm not worried about that. I'm so grateful to you for calling for help."

Dylan looked down at the floor, not feeling deserving of the praise. "We brought you some magazines. In case you get bored." He placed the stack on the short portable table beside the bed.

"Thank you. How thoughtful. This reminds me, would you be able to retrieve my mail and newspaper for the next few days? I'll give you the garage code and you can just put everything in the house."

"Yeah. Sure." Dylan was glad to help out. Mr. Lyman wrote his code on a slip of paper and handed it to Dylan.

"I'm going to the cafeteria to get some coffee. Mr. Lyman would you like anything?" Mrs. Fisher asked.

"I'd love some coffee. Black."

Mrs. Fisher squeezed Dylan's shoulder as she walked by and left the room.

"Please, sit." Mr. Lyman nodded toward the reclining chair beside his bed.

Dylan sat down and leaned back. The blue vinyl was stiff and cold. He wished the TV was on so he had something to look at. He needed to ask Mr. Lyman about the wind crystal and Mile High, but he wasn't sure how to bring it up.

"I'm glad you got your geocache placed before the accident." Mr. Lyman smoothed the blanket across his legs.

This was Dylan's chance. "I didn't tell you what was in the cache."

"You said it was a rock."

"Technically it was, but really it was another crystal. Well, half of one. With the wind symbol."

Mr. Lyman sat up straighter in bed. "Is that so? Where did you find it?"

"In Boulder. The owner of the geocoin cache, Mile High, told me where it was. I found it and returned it to the site at Chatfield State Park so he can get it. I just hope he does." Dylan watched Mr. Lyman for any sign that he was Mile High.

"Did you notify him that the crystal is in his original cache?"

Dylan nodded.

"Well, then I'm sure he'll get it eventually."

Dylan focused on Mr. Lyman's last word—*eventually*. Was he talking about himself? Did he say that because he wouldn't be able to get to the crystal until he was out of the hospital?

"So I guess this means the four elemental crystals really do exist. That's powerful knowledge. Are you sure you can trust this Mile High?"

"I don't know, but it would be nice to find out who it is." Dylan glanced up at Mr. Lyman, waiting for answer.

"I'm sure when the time is right, Mile High will reveal himself, or herself." Mr. Lyman smiled. "How much of this does Colonel Thornton know? He was certainly interested in my book."

"None of it. Tera, Kari, EJ, and I are the only ones who know about the crystals. Well, and now you."

Mr. Lyman took a deep breath. "I know all this crystal stuff seems exciting, Dylan, but there are people who take the science of the creation stone very seriously. I'm not telling you what to do, but I think it'd be in your best interest not to pursue the crystals any further. I know you have the earth crystal, and that secret is safe with me. But please, don't let it get into the wrong hands."

Dylan's mouth dropped open. There were those words again—like a warning signal. Did Mr. Lyman know about 4E Labs? "Mr. Lyman, are you M--"

His mom walked back into the room. "One coffee, black, at your service." She set Mr. Lyman's cup on the portable table.

"Thank you." Mr. Lyman inhaled. "It reminds me of home."

Dylan slouched in the recliner. Now he wouldn't get to ask Mr. Lyman if he was really Mile High.

"Have the doctors given you any idea when you'll be able to go home?" Mrs. Fisher took a sip of her coffee.

"Given my age, they're running a few extra tests, but it shouldn't be more than a couple days."

"Make sure to let me know. I'll be the one to bail you out of this place." Mrs. Fisher winked.

The nurse wearing the dark red scrubs walked into the room. "Time to take your vitals."

Mrs. Fisher moved out of the nurse's way. "We'll get out of your hair. I'll check in on you tomorrow, and Dylan will check on your house and get the mail and paper." She gave Dylan a look that meant, 'right?'

"Uh, yeah, don't worry. I'll take care of everything." Dylan got up from the recliner.

Mr. Lyman stopped him, placing a hand on his forearm. "Dylan, thanks for being such a good friend."

Dylan nodded and followed his mom out of the room, but his mind raced through all the comments he and Tera had exchanged with Mile High. She had asked if Mile High was a 'friend or foe.' Did Mr. Lyman's comment mean he was the 'friend?'

Dylan didn't say much in the car on the way home. The first thing he wanted to do was check and see if Mile High had responded to his post. Doubtful, especially if Mile High was Mr. Lyman.

As they turned down their street, his mom slowed down and pulled into Mr. Lyman's driveway. "Why don't you hop out here and grab the mail and paper and put it inside like Mr. Lyman asked. I'll meet you at home."

Dylan got out of the car and walked to the bank of mailboxes across the street. He grabbed Mr. Lyman's mail and went back to his driveway, bending over to pick up the orange plastic baggie with the evening's newspaper. He walked up to the garage, flipped up the cover on the code panel, and typed in the four numbers written on the slip of paper Mr. Lyman had given him.

The garage door slowly creaked open. An empty space sat where the Prius should be, but the walls were lined with metal shelves that held tools, boxes, buckets, shovels, and rakes. It was like an entire hardware store in Mr. Lyman's garage.

Dylan turned the knob on the door that led into the house. It was unlocked. He walked past a small laundry room and down a short hall. It didn't seem like the same house without the radio playing in the background and the smell of coffee coming from the kitchen.

He got to the living room and dropped the mail and paper on the desk. He turned toward the display cabinet and stopped, stunned by what he saw. The light in the top was glowing, but the cabinet door was open, and every rock inside was gone. Dylan gasped—someone must have stolen them.

The earth crystal! That's what the thief must have been after. Was the burglar still in the house? Dylan held his breath, listening for movement. The house was silent. He hurried to the front door and noticed it wasn't closed all the way. He peered out, but didn't see anybody or any cars parked in the street. The thief must be long gone. He closed the door and locked the dead bolt. Should he call the police? They probably wouldn't care about a bunch of stolen rocks. And if he did call, he'd have to list everything that was stolen, and he didn't want to mention the crystal. No, he could take care of this himself and explain it to Mr. Lyman later.

Dylan walked back to the display cabinet, closed the door, and turned off the light in the top. The sight of the empty case made him angry, and there was only one explanation for the theft—4E Labs. Somehow they found out Mr. Lyman had the crystal. But what they didn't know was that Dylan had switched it. Did the thief think they had the real crystal? Would they discover it was a fake and come after him?

The next thought made Dylan's stomach seize. If the thief thought they had gotten the earth crystal back, that meant they needed the catalyst. And the catalyst was Tera.

He ran out into Mr. Lyman's garage, punched in the code to close the door, and sprinted down the street to Tera's house. He hoped he wasn't too late.

Chapter Sixteen

Dylan pounded his fist on Tera's front door. He peered in the side windows and saw a light shining from the kitchen. She should be home. His nerves eased a little when he recognized her silhouette move down the hall.

Tera opened the door and smiled at Dylan. She stepped onto the porch and opened her arms. At the same time, he leaned toward her and they bumped foreheads.

"Oh sorry!" Dylan gave her an awkward pat on the back.

Tera rubbed the spot where they had collided. "My fault." She chuckled and gave him another smile. "I'm so glad you're okay. Kari told me everything. How is Mr. Lyman?"

"He's fine, but someone broke into his house and took all the rocks. The display case is empty. I think they were looking for the earth crystal, and I think it was 4E Labs." Even in the fading daylight, Dylan could see Tera's face lose its color.

"How would 4E Labs know Mr. Lyman had the earth crystal? Do you think he told somebody about it?"

Dylan shook his head. "He told me that secret was safe."

"What if the thief wasn't after the earth crystal? What if they were after the wind crystal?"

Dylan gave Tera a skeptical look. “How would 4E Labs even know about the wind crystal?”

“What if they’ve been following the blog comments, and they think Mr. Lyman is Mile High, just like we do?”

The thought that anyone could see their blog comments had crossed Dylan’s mind, but the blog hardly had any followers, and the chances of 4E Labs finding it seemed pretty slim. “The good news is I still have the earth crystal. And we’ll find out who Mile High is soon enough. But, there is some bad news.”

Tera sat down on the front step. “I already know. As soon as Kari mentioned the wind storm, I figured I had something to do with it.”

Dylan sat down next to her. “I’m sorry I ever asked you to hold the crystal. I promise it won’t happen again.” He waited for her to say ‘it’s okay,’ but she stayed silent. Dylan stared straight ahead, watching the bright orange sun dip completely behind the mountains. Tera’s porch light clicked on.

She spoke quietly. “I think as long as 4E Labs and the crystals are out there, I’ll always be at risk. Which is why you need to get the wind crystal back. Both halves.”

Dylan turned back toward Tera, stunned. “What? I thought you wanted me to be done with the crystals!”

“Well, now I want you to find them. All of them. That’s the only way we’ll ever be done.”

A quick laugh of disbelief escaped Dylan’s mouth. “How am I supposed to do that?”

Tera finally faced him. “Post another comment to Mile High. Tell him you think you’ve discovered the catalyst for the wind crystal, but you need the entire crystal to test it out and make sure. Tell him you want to meet with him in person. If he brings the crystal, you'll bring the catalyst."

Dylan stood up, staring down at Tera. "That's insane! You want the two of us to meet Mile High with the crystal?" Flashbacks of Frank kidnapping Tera and the earth crystal filled his head. He wasn't about to put her in the same position again.

Tera tugged on Dylan's shirt, signaling him to sit back down. "Assuming Mile High is Mr. Lyman, we won't be at risk. We can tell him everything. I bet he'd even be willing to help us find the other two crystals."

Dylan sat down again. "Maybe. I need to talk to him, especially about the break-in. He'll be home in two days." He looked at Tera out of the corner of his eye. "Are you sure you don't want to bring your dad in on it now?"

"Positive. Not until we know who Mile High is."

That wasn't the answer Dylan was hoping for. "Then keep an eye out for any strangers or 4E Lab vans driving around." He stood up and smoothed the back of his shorts. "I better get home. I'll talk to you later."

Tera didn't get up. "See ya."

When Dylan got home his mom and dad were in the living room watching TV.

"Everything okay at Mr. Lyman's?" Mrs. Fisher asked.

"Uh-huh." Dylan hurried through the room on his way upstairs, avoiding lying to his parents' faces. Jordan's room was dark, which meant she must be out. It was Saturday night, and she never stayed home on a Saturday night. He went into the office to grab his iPod and noticed the GeoTalk blog site on the screen. It was still up from the last comment he posted. Out of habit he clicked the refresh button. Nothing. His disappointment surprised him. But it also strengthened his belief that Mr. Lyman was Mile High.

He leaned over the keyboard and typed another comment. *Mile High, I discovered the catalyst for the wind crystal, but need it back to try it out. Can we meet? You bring the crystal, I'll bring the catalyst.* Dylan hit send, closed out the web page, and with his iPod in hand, went down to his room and laid on his bed to listen to music. He just wanted a break from all the craziness.

Dylan pedals his bike along the winding road leading from Chatfield State Park. He tries downshifting to make it easier, but the gears won't budge. He pumps his legs a few more times then stops, coasting along the road's center line. He grips the bike's middle bar with his knees and lets go of the handlebars. He closes his eyes for a second, the sensation of flying overtaking him.

A gust of wind slaps him in the face, and he leans backward, grappling for the handlebars. The front wheel wobbles, and Dylan's arms struggle to steady it. Directly ahead a swirling mass of dust spins toward him. It's the size of his house, blocking the entire road. He squeezes the brake handle and skids to a stop. The tornado continues to barrel toward him. Dylan drops his bike in the middle of the road and runs toward the ditch on the side. His foot slides on a rock and he tumbles, rolling sideways down into the ditch. The tornado thunders over him. He covers his head with his arms as ferocious winds blast above. He hears the sound of screeching metal and looks up to catch a glimpse of his bike caught in the twister, its handlebars folded in like a pretzel.

Then the tornado spits the bike out, and it lands inches away, a heap of scrap metal. The giant dust devil slows down and disappears like fog. A ray of sunlight shines down on the bike, and Dylan notices something glinting in a wheel spoke. He crawls over to it and grabs a glittering gold chain. Hanging off the end is the wind crystal, complete with both halves.

Dylan woke up from the dream with a jolt. His room was dark, and it took him several seconds to realize that none of it had happened, even though his forehead was damp with sweat. One of the earbuds from his iPod stuck to his neck. He sat up and looked at the clock. It was after midnight. His mom must have turned off his lights before she went to bed. Jordan's muffled voice floated under the door. She was home, talking on the phone.

Dylan rolled over and closed his eyes, hoping he could fall back asleep. But he had such a rush from the dream he knew it'd never happen. He got out of bed and went downstairs to watch TV. He flipped through a bunch of channels and stopped on an infomercial for a blender that could grind a brick. He could imagine all the things he and EJ could find to grind up—blocks of wood, cement chunks, or even the metal from the bottom of Jordan's old tap shoes.

An hour later he turned off the TV and wandered into the kitchen. He grabbed two Oreos and poured himself a glass of milk, which he took upstairs. He went into the office and sat down in front of the computer. The bright bluish glow from the monitor in the dark room was like staring at the sun. It took a few seconds for his eyes to adjust so he could see the keyboard. He opened a new web page and typed "elemental symbols" in the search engine box. Lists of sites and images filled the screen. He scanned the pictures until he saw some he recognized: the same triangle symbols that were in Mr. Lyman's book. He clicked "print" and typed in a new search for "creation stone." Some sites called it the "philosopher's stone", and each one he clicked on talked about it as a legend ancient scientists believed could turn metals into gold and silver. It was also believed to make people live longer.

Dylan popped an entire Oreo into his mouth and chewed slowly. He just couldn't figure out what 4E Labs planned to do with the creation stone if they ever got all four crystals. Maybe Mile High knew? If only Mile High would send him a comment back. He opened another page and typed in the GeoTalk blog site. He scrolled down and stopped, nearly choking on his Oreo.

Dear Cache is King, I have both halves of the crystal and will meet you and the catalyst. Just tell me when and where.

Dylan's heart thumped inside his chest as a knot of fear lodged in his stomach. Mr. Lyman was definitely *not* Mile High. What had he gotten himself into? What had he gotten Tera into? He needed to tell her about this. He pushed the chair away from the keyboard and stood up before he realized it was the middle of the night. Mr. Paine would kill him if he called Tera right now. He could send her a text instead, and she'd see it first thing in the morning.

He crept downstairs to the phone charging station in the kitchen and typed in his message. MILE HIGH WROTE BACK. NOT MR LYMAN. HAS FULL WIND CRYSTAL. WANTS TO MEET. He sent the message and paced around the kitchen. The full moon shining through the windows gave him enough light to avoid bumping into the kitchen chairs. He stopped and gazed out into the back yard. The moon reflected off the creek water that ran behind his house. The place where it all started—where he first found the earth crystal and where he first met Tera.

That was it! He could meet Mile High in the creek. If anything went wrong, he'd be close to home and could make a run for it. He'd be ready this time.

Dylan went back upstairs and slid into the office chair. He pulled up a GPS web site and typed in his address, resulting in a set of coordinates. Next he typed a new message to Mile High. *Meet me at the following location on Monday at 4:00 pm. I'll be waiting by the creek.*

His hand shook as he clicked the submit button. There was no going back now. And there was no way he'd be able to get any sleep tonight either.

Chapter Seventeen

"Dylan. Dylan, wake up."

Dylan moaned and swatted his mom away as she shook his leg to jostle him awake.

"Dylan, it's ten o'clock. I let you sleep through breakfast, but now you need to get up. Besides, Tera is waiting for you downstairs."

At the mention of Tera, Dylan's eyes popped open. She must have finally read his text from last night. "I'm up, I'm up." He scrambled out of bed and put on the same crumpled T-shirt he wore the day before.

"You were up late watching TV last night, weren't you?" Mrs. Fisher accused.

"I couldn't sleep." Dylan smoothed down his bed head by rubbing his hand over his hair.

"I expect your homework to be done before you go anywhere today," Mrs. Fisher called after him as he ran downstairs.

Tera greeted him in the entryway. "Sorry. Didn't mean to get you out of bed."

"That's okay." Dylan tried smoothing out his wrinkled shirt and realized he was still wearing plaid pajama pants. "Did you get my text?"

Tera's gaze fell to the floor. "Yeah. Can we go outside? We need to talk."

Alarms went off in Dylan's head. Whenever his parents told him "we need to talk" it only meant one thing—he was in trouble. He followed Tera outside onto his front porch and closed the door behind him. "What's up?"

"I accidentally left my phone in my dad's office last night. He was up late, or I guess early, working, and he sort of…well, he read your text about Mile High and the wind crystal." Tera closed her eyes like she was ashamed.

Dylan was too horrified to speak. His face ignited with heat like he had just been caught in the worst lie of his life. "What did your dad say?" he whispered.

"I had to tell him what your text meant. I told him about Mile High, about the four elements, and about how you found the wind crystal. I even told him I'm a catalyst for it."

"And the earth crystal…?"

Tera looked at him through her long lashes, her green eyes sparkling. "I may have left that part out."

For the first time, Dylan was relieved Mr. Paine didn't know he had the earth crystal. It was the only thing he still had some control over. "What now?"

"Now my dad wants to take over. He wants to know when and where you're meeting Mile High."

"Did you tell him?"

Tera looked at him like he had two heads. "How could I tell him? I don't even know."

Dylan forgot he hadn't told her that part yet. "I set it up for--"

"No!" Tera covered her ears. "If you don't tell me, then I can't lie to my dad about it. I'll just say you refused. Not much he can do about that."

"But I need you to come with me when I meet Mile High. That was the deal. He brings the crystal, I bring the catalyst."

Tera walked in a circle around the porch then stopped. "What if you still can?"

"You mean you'll come with me?"

"Not exactly. You didn't tell Mile High who the catalyst was, just as long as you show up with a girl."

Dylan wasn't following her thinking. "If you don't come with me, then who will?" His sister came to mind, but there was no way he was going to try and explain something this complicated to her.

Tera stared at him like she was waiting for him to figure it out. "Hello! I'm talking about Kari!"

"Ohhh. Yeah. That makes sense. But there's one problem. What happens when Mile High figures out Kari isn't the catalyst?"

"Mile High doesn't know what happens when a crystal is activated. Kari can make something up. And as long as you can get the crystal from Mile High, you're in the clear."

Dylan mulled this over for a minute. It could actually work. "But what about your dad? He'll freak out if he finds out I went ahead and met Mile High without him. And I thought part of the plan was to let him catch Mile High."

"When are you meeting him?"

"Monday after school." Dylan wasn't sure how much information Tera wanted about it.

"If Mile High turns out to be someone from 4E Labs, text me a 9-1-1 message with your location. I'll make sure my dad is home."

Dylan nodded and then thought of something else. "There's one other thing we need to do. Get Kari to go along with all this." He worried she'd change the plan and try to take over.

Tera flashed him a confident smile. "Leave that to me. I know exactly what to say."

* * *

"I can totally pretend to be the catalyst!" Kari seemed even more excited than when she had won her soccer tournament.

"Shhh! Not so loud." Dylan looked over both his shoulders to make sure nobody in the school cafeteria was paying attention to their conversation.

EJ picked up a cheesy clump of beef nachos from his tray and shoved it into his mouth.

Kari gave him a disgusted look across the table before turning her attention back to Tera. "How does it work, do I need to rub the crystal? Pretend like it shocks me or something?"

Tera took a long sip through the straw sticking out of her milk carton. "You don't need to pretend to activate the crystal, just let Mile High believe you're the catalyst. If he asks what it feels like, tell him it's kind of a tingling, pulling sensation."

Kari stared at Tera for several seconds then looked down at her hands as if she was checking them for marker stains. "I think I know what you mean."

"Did your dad grill you about my meeting with Mile High?" Dylan didn't want Tera to get into any more trouble with her dad than she already had.

"It was like an interrogation. He sat me down at the kitchen table and paced back and forth, firing off questions. I told him I didn't know when or where you were meeting, which is true. Then he told me I wasn't allowed to go anywhere after school this week until the situation was resolved. He actually said that."

EJ wiped his mouth with his T-shirt sleeve, leaving a grease smear across his shoulder. "So you're grounded. That sucks."

"If my dad won't let me out of his sight, at least he'll be around if Dylan needs him."

EJ let out a deep burp. "Dude, you need to do a grab n' go; nab the crystal from Mile High and run like crazy. Hey, maybe I should come with you. We could run a quarterback sneak. I am the fastest player on my football team."

EJ was fast. Dylan had never beaten him in a foot race. He pictured himself grabbing the wind crystal necklace out of Mile High's hands and pitching it to EJ who would tuck it under his arm like a football and race out of the creek. Dylan smiled at the thought until he realized he'd be the one left behind to deal with Mile High.

"You don't really want to come, do you?" Kari looked at EJ like she had just eaten a bad nacho.

EJ gave her a sly smile. "Maybe I do. When is this secret rendezvous?"

Dylan glanced at Tera before answering. "Today after school. That's all I can tell you for now."

"Aw, man! Can't. Football practice. Looks like you win, Scary Kar--"

Kari shot him the evil eye. "Are you sure you want

to call me that?"

EJ hunched down on his side of the lunch table. "Sorry, *Johansen*."

Kari sat up straighter with a satisfied look on her face. "Dylan, we really do need some type of plan. And signals, you know, like if we need to make a quick exit. I could hold up one finger if everything is on the up and up and two fingers if we need to bolt."

Dylan's stomach rolled, and he wasn't sure if it was from the nachos or from nerves. Until now, he hadn't really thought about how he was going to get the wind crystal from Mile High. He had just been excited that he'd finally know who Mile High was. But he was a little disappointed it wasn't Mr. Lyman. That would have been a lot easier. He remembered his mom was picking up Mr. Lyman up from the hospital this afternoon. Dylan planned to tell him all about Mile High after the meeting. "Let's figure it out on the way home from school."

The kids got up from the table, threw away their trash, and stacked their trays on the cart by the school kitchen.

"I'll meet you outside the main doors after school," Kari said.

EJ unwrapped a candy bar from his pocket and took a bite, leaving a string of caramel hanging off his chin. "Good luck today. I hope you catch the bad guy."

Dylan piled his tray on top of the others. "Maybe it won't be a bad guy."

"Haven't you ever seen a movie? They always turn out to be bad guys." EJ crammed the rest of the candy bar in his mouth and headed down the hall.

Now Dylan's stomach really didn't feel good. He

turned and found Tera standing behind him.

"Don't listen to EJ. I'm sure everything will be fine. I've seen all the comments from Mile High, and I don't think it's anyone from 4E Labs. I wouldn't let you go if I did." Tera smiled.

"I just don't want a repeat of what happened with…"

"Frank. It's okay. You can say his name around me. And there's no way anything like that will ever happen again. You know what to watch out for now. And Kari's smart. She won't let anything happen to her." Tera looked at the floor.

"Hey, you're smart too. It wasn't your fault you know." Dylan touched her elbow.

Tera looked up. "I'll just be glad when you find out who Mile High is, get the crystal, and we can turn everything over to my dad. I'm tired of keeping everything a secret from him."

"Really? Give him *both* crystals?"

Tera nodded.

Dylan's stomach suddenly felt much better.

Chapter Eighteen

Dylan paced in the entryway of his house, stopping every few seconds to glance out the front window. Where was Kari? He told her to be at his house at three forty-five. He checked the time on his cell phone. It was three forty-seven. They were supposed to meet Mile High at the creek at four o'clock. The plan wouldn't work without her.

At three fifty he texted her. WHERE R U? His phone vibrated seconds later.

FINISHING HOMEWORK. MEET U OUT BACK IN 5.

Dylan should have known Kari would change the plan. JUST HURRY! He shoved his phone in his pocket and went into the kitchen. His mom was sitting at the table with her laptop.

"I'll be out back," Dylan said.

"Don't go far. We're eating right at five. Jordan has a dance performance tonight." Mrs. Fisher's eyes didn't move off the computer screen.

"I don't have to go though, right?"

His mom looked at him over the top of her computer. "It'd be nice if you showed your sister some support."

Dylan let out a half snort. "Dance squad isn't exactly a competitive sport. Maybe if she played a real sport like soccer or volleyball, then I'd go."

Mrs. Fisher gave him a disapproving look. "Either way, be home by five. Oh, I picked up Mr. Lyman from the hospital today. He wanted me to thank you for taking care of his house."

Dylan froze. He had almost forgotten about Mr. Lyman's rocks! He needed to tell him what happened. But it'd have to wait. After he met with Mile High, he'd go to Mr. Lyman's house and explain everything. At least he'd have a good excuse not to go to Jordan's recital.

Dylan opened the door in the kitchen leading to the deck and went outside. The breeze seemed a little cooler, like fall was waiting to take summer's place. He headed into the backyard and made his way down the grassy hill to the creek. Its banks were bare patches of cracked dirt, and the water was only as deep as a bathtub. The hot summer had turned this once raging river into a wading pool.

The trees surrounding the creek were still thick with leaves, but their ends had browned and curled in the sun. Patches of light scattered through the branches. Dylan walked between the trees, making sure no one hid behind them. The only sounds came from the trickling water and traffic in the distance.

He came to the hollow log where he first found the crystal earth cache and sat down, straddling it. He picked at a piece of peeling bark while he waited for Kari. And Mile High. A chill scurried up his spine, forcing a shiver through his upper body. Could he really pull this off? Would Mile High give him the wind crystal? Would he believe Kari was the catalyst? Tera and Kari seemed so confident, but he was second guessing everything.

Maybe he should call Mr. Paine and tell him about the meeting and ask him to come to the creek. He'd be able to handle Mile High.

Then a new thought slammed Dylan. What if Mile High was the one who broke into Mr. Lyman's house? What if Mile High knew about Tera, Dylan, and the earth crystal? What if they were all in danger?

He climbed off the log and headed back toward his yard. Tera had already said she was going to tell her dad about the earth crystal so it wouldn't matter if he beat her to it.

Dylan didn't get far before he saw Kari running down the hill toward him.

"I told you I'd be here in five minutes. I wasn't going to ditch you. I'm totally ready for this." Her cheeks were pink from running.

Dylan wasn't about to admit he was ready to give up. Seeing Kari's excitement brought a new surge of hope. "Okay. Let's go over the plan again. When Mile High shows up, we need to make sure he's the one who posted all the blog messages."

Kari walked beside Dylan back to the creek. "And how do we do that?"

"Only Mile High knows where the 'Wind Beneath My Wings' cache was hidden. Once that's clear, then we have to make sure Mile High isn't working for 4E Labs." They stopped when they reached the edge of the creek bank.

"That one will be harder to prove," Kari said.

"If Mile High is involved with 4E Labs, then he'll probably know about Frank and the Wyoming company that was digging up the mine."

Kari let out a big sigh. "I'll let you worry about that. I need to focus on convincing Mile High I'm the catalyst and get him to give me the crystal."

"What are you going to do?"

"Tera gave me some pointers. I'm going to pretend like I feel a huge wind storm coming on and make a big deal out of everyone running for cover. Then you and I can head straight to the Paine's for safety."

Dylan thought about Tera's promise to tell her dad everything. "Actually, Mr. Paine will already be involved. I'm supposed to text Tera as soon as I find out who Mile High is, tell her where we're at, and then she'll bring her dad here to confront Mile High. It should all work out."

Kari scrunched her face, which usually meant she didn't agree. "What if Mile High is a complete stranger and we don't find out his name or who he works for? He could easily take off before Mr. Paine gets here, especially if he figures out I'm not the catalyst. Then our chance is blown." She paced in front of the hollow log. "What we need is leverage. Something to make sure Mile High does what we want."

Dylan watched Kari, who looked like a tiger pacing its cage at the zoo. "What sort of…leverage?"

Kari stopped. Her face lit up. "We could tell him we know where another crystal is."

"But we don't."

"Mile High doesn't know that," Kari said with a slow, sarcastic tone. "If we tell him we know the coordinates for the fire or water crystal, then it'll keep him interested."

"Unless Mile High already knows where they are, then he'd figure out we were lying about it."

Kari shook her head. "Even better! If Mile High does know where another crystal is, maybe he'd give away a clue and we could find out where."

Now it was Dylan's turn to pace. "I think we should stick to the plan—figure out who Mile High is and get the wind crystal." Why did everyone always try to change things? First Tera made him promise not to say anything to her dad, and now she was willing to give him both crystals. And Kari wanted to throw in this new idea of pretending to know where another crystal was. It was like everybody wanted to be captain of the kickball team at once.

Kari held up her hands in surrender. "Okay, you're right. We'll stick to the plan. I won't say anything about other crystals. But if you did know where they were, would you go after them?"

Dylan plunked down on the log and sighed. "Yeah. I would. I think I'd do anything to keep the crystals away from 4E Labs and keep Tera…I mean, Tera's secret, safe."

Kari sat down on the log beside him. Dylan picked up a leaf off the ground and twirled it by the stem. He avoiding looking at Kari, hoping she wouldn't say anything about his feelings for Tera.

"I wonder what it's like," she said.

"You wonder what *what's* like?"

"What it's like to be a catalyst. To be the only person in the world who has that power. I mean, Tera can create earthquakes for crying out loud. And she can probably make a tornado spin up out of nothing. But she seems so calm about it all. Has she talked to you about it very much?"

Now Dylan looked at Kari. "Who, me? No. Why would she talk to me about it?"

"Because you guys are, you know, really close. And because you two have gone through all this crystal stuff together."

Dylan huffed. "I would think you'd be the one she'd talk to. You guys are best friends."

"I know, but every time I try to bring it up, she just shrugs it off and says she got stuck with 'bad genes.' Obviously she blames her mom."

Dylan had never asked Tera how she felt about being a catalyst to the crystals. Now he was glad he hadn't. It sounded like she didn't want to talk about it, so he made a mental note not to bring it up.

"Hey, you want to see what Tera showed me?" Kari slid off the log and turned to face Dylan. She clasped her hands in front of her and closed her eyes.

"Are you praying?" Dylan snickered.

Kari opened one eye. "No, I'm pretending like I'm holding the crystal." She closed her eye again and her face turned serious. After several seconds she opened her eyes, tilted her head to the sky, and circled her arms above her head like she was swirling the air.

Dylan let out a cackle. "What is that? You look like you're doing a bad modern dance. Did Tera tell you to do that with your arms?"

Kari kept going. "No, this part is my own addition. It gives it more of a magical feel, don't you think?"

"No, I don't. You look like a total nut job."

Kari stopped and put her hands on her hips, like she was ready to read Dylan the riot act. She opened her mouth and quickly closed it, then stood straight at attention, staring past Dylan.

He turned around and saw someone in a red jacket walking toward them through the trees. His stomach knotted and he scrambled off the log, falling in line beside Kari.

"Is it Mile High?" she whispered.

Dylan glanced at his watch. Four o'clock. Right on time. "I'm guessing so."

"Can you tell who it is?"

The person wore a baseball hat, so Dylan couldn't see his face. But Mile High was tall-- and thin. He walked quickly, right toward them. Dylan's heart felt like a bass drum beating in his chest. He didn't take his focus off Mile High, whose head was bent down as he maneuvered around the trees. Finally, he reached Dylan and Kari, stopped, and looked directly at them.

Mile High was a woman.

Chapter Nineteen

Dylan blinked several times, making sure his eyes weren't playing tricks on him. But the person standing in front of him was definitely a woman. Wisps of red hair stuck out from underneath her baseball hat, and her eyes were as green as the center of the earth crystal. She looked familiar even though Dylan was sure he had never seen her before. He and Kari glanced at each other but didn't say anything.

"Are one of you Cache is King?" the woman asked, looking back and forth between Dylan and Kari.

Dylan gave a single wave of his hand. "I am. Are you Mile High?"

The woman nodded. "Sure am. You seem younger than I was expecting."

Dylan didn't say he wasn't expecting someone so… female. "Who were you expecting? I figured the cache was really meant for someone else."

Mile High didn't respond right away. "Let's just say you aren't the only one looking for the crystals."

Heat shimmied up Dylan's back even though a breeze blew through the trees. Was she referring to 4E Labs? He needed to find out whose side she was on. "Can you prove you're really Mile High?"

The woman raised an eyebrow in surprise. "You're

thorough. I like that. Here's my proof. I went to the Wind Beneath My Wings cache located in Chatfield State Park and retrieved the half of the wind crystal you left there, which was located underneath the garbage receptacle near the model airplane runway. The hidden camera was a nice touch by the way." She smiled and slipped her hands inside her jacket pockets.

Dylan wanted to kick himself for not being able to retrieve the camera before the meeting. But she was definitely Mile High. Now he needed to know if she worked for 4E Labs. "How do you know about the crystals?"

"I think I should be the one asking you that question."

Dylan had heard his mom use that same tone, so he knew he had to come up with an answer. And when it came to his mom, honesty was always the best policy. "I found it by accident. It was in a cache right here in that hollow log."

Mile High stared at the log for several seconds. "How did you find out what it could do?" This time she looked at Kari.

"Oh, well, that was by accident too," Kari said.

Dylan gave Kari an intense look, hoping she wouldn't give away too much too soon.

"And how did you find out there were more crystals?" Mile High asked.

"I read about them in a book. It didn't talk about the crystals exactly, but about the four elements and how early scientists believed they made up the Creation Stone." Dylan didn't know why he felt so comfortable telling Mile High about all this. "Since I knew the first crystal controlled the earth, I figured there must be crystals for the other elements too."

"You're very intelligent." Mile High's voice was full of praise. "So what do you know about 4E Labs involvement?"

Dylan couldn't hide his surprise at Mile High's direct question. "I know they're the bad guys. They're after all four crystals and the catalyst. I just don't know why."

"You're right. They are the bad guys. And I'm trying to figure out why they're after the crystals too. Which is why I'm glad we can work together." Mile High took her hand out of her coat pocket and extended it toward Dylan.

Satisfied with her answer, Dylan took a step forward to shake hands with Mile High, but Kari put her arm out and blocked him.

"Show us the wind crystal first," Kari said. "Both halves."

Dylan lowered his arm, surprised by Kari's bold demand. But he realized she was right. He shouldn't trust Mile High so easily. He had just been anxious to get this whole thing over with.

"Fair enough." Mile High reached into the top of her jacket and pulled out a gold chain hanging around her neck. On the end of it hung a crystal pendant. She turned it over, showing Dylan and Kari that it was complete on both sides before letting it rest against the outside of her coat.

"How did you get the two halves together?" Dylan asked, leaning forward to get a better look.

"They fit like puzzle pieces," Mile High said.

Kari planted her hands on her hips. "I want to see it

for myself. It could be a fake."

Mile High placed her hand around the crystal. "I assure you it's not a fake. But, there is only one way to find out. We'd need to see what happens when the crystal comes in contact with the catalyst."

"Then let's find out," Kari said, holding out her hand.

Mile High shook her head. "The real catalyst."

Heat rushed to Dylan's face, and he was sure red blotches were popping up like pimples. He stared at Kari, waiting for her answer.

"I am the real catalyst," she said, her voice higher than normal.

Mile High gave her a sympathetic smile. "I appreciate what you're trying to do. I think it's noble of you to protect your friend. But the only way we're going to know with one hundred percent certainty that this is, in fact, the wind crystal, is if we try it out with the real catalyst. And we all know the real catalyst is the captain's daughter."

"How do you--" Dylan started.

Mile High held up her hand, cutting him off. "When you've spent as much time as I have researching the crystals, you know who all the important players are."

Dylan couldn't help let his mouth drop open in shock.

"Don't worry. I want to protect her as much as you do. But I need to confirm she's the catalyst. I need you to bring her here."

"No way," Dylan said. "Not gonna happen."

"Then I'm not giving you the crystal." Mile High slipped the pendant back into the neck of her jacket.

Dylan boldly stepped toward Mile High. “But we had a deal.”

“Yes, we did. I brought the crystal, and you were supposed to bring the catalyst. You didn’t uphold your end of the deal.”

“We didn’t know if we could trust you, or if we still can! You might be working for 4E Labs. How are we supposed to know?” Kari’s voice echoed through the creek.

“I told you, I’m on your side. I don’t want 4E Labs getting the crystals any more than you do!”

Dylan closed his eyes, trying to block out the arguing. Every exchange with Mile High was like blowing another breath into a balloon that was about to pop. "Stop it! Just stop!”

Kari and Mile High fell silent and turned toward Dylan.

“You’re right. She isn’t the catalyst.” Dylan pointed at Kari. “But I’m not going to just hand Tera over to you. Not until you give me one good reason why I should call her out here.”

Mile High closed her eyes and took a deep breath before opening them again and sitting down on the hollow log. “Because I know Tera’s parents and worked with them until her mom’s…death.”

“What do you mean worked with them?” Kari asked.

“I was on the military research team that was trying to find a catalyst for the crystal. After Hannah died, I quit. I didn’t want to do it anymore. Then I got a phone call last year from Captain Paine asking if I’d consider picking it up again. He told me he was tracking the crystal and back on the project.”

Dylan shook his head. "Wait a minute. You're working with Tera's dad?"

"That's who the geocoin was meant for. It was the safest way to communicate. When I got your blog message I thought I was dealing with someone from 4E Labs. That's why I had you go to the pawn shop. The owner is a friend of mine and I knew he'd tell me who came to retrieve it. Captain Paine said you had been involved with the earth crystal, so as soon as I heard a kid came into the pawn shop, I knew I could trust you." Mile High smiled.

"If Mr. Paine knew I was meeting you, then why didn't he let Tera come?" Dylan asked.

"Safety precaution. In case someone from 4E Labs was monitoring the blog, he didn't want Tera to be here."

"Then why did you just say you wanted her here?" Kari's anger hadn't let up.

"I just wanted you to realize I knew you were lying."

Dylan paced in a small circle, trying to think through all the information. "So did you break into Mr. Lyman's house looking for the earth crystal?"

Mile High's head snapped up. "Who's Mr. Lyman? What are you talking about?"

"He's my neighbor, and he's a geologist. I had secretly given him the earth crystal for safe keeping in his display cabinet. Even Mr. Paine didn't know about it. Then I replaced it with a fake one. The other day someone broke in and stole it. I figured it must have been someone from 4E Labs."

Mile High stood up. "Did you tell Mr. Paine about the break-in?"

"I haven't even told Mr. Lyman yet. He's been in

the hospital. We got into a car accident on the way back from geocaching. It was caused by a wind storm that we think Tera might have activated after touching half the wind crystal."

"Maybe 4E Labs has found a new thug since Frank's...disappearance."

Dylan and Kari glanced at each other.

"If Tera was able to set off a wind storm after activating only half the crystal, I can only imagine what might happen if she got a hold of the whole thing." Mile High sighed. "I want you to give both the wind and earth crystals to Captain Paine. He's the only one who can truly keep them safe and protect Tera."

Mile High unzipped her jacket, exposing the pendant. The golden triangle suspended in the middle of the crystal glittered like fool's gold. She reached around the back of her neck to remove the necklace. As she did, Dylan glimpsed the multicolored logo stitched on her shirt.

It said "4E Labs."

Chapter Twenty

No. Not again, Dylan thought, recognizing the four interlocking triangles that made 4E Lab's logo. He looked at Kari to see if she had noticed it too, but Kari seemed focused on the necklace. Dylan didn't know what to do—should he grab the necklace and run? Confront Mile High about lying? At least he hadn't texted Tera yet and told her to come to the creek. She was safe. For now.

Mile High gathered the necklace in her hand and held it out to Dylan. He opened his palm, face up, and she dropped the heavy pendant into it. The smooth surface of the crystal was warm from laying against Mile High's neck. Holding it securely in his hand gave Dylan renewed confidence.

"You said you were in research. Who do you work for?" He narrowed his eyes at Mile High as if daring her to lie again.

Mile High gave him a questioning look. "I didn't say who I worked for."

"I'm not surprised. I wouldn't either if I worked for the enemy."

"Dylan, what are you talking about?" Kari whispered.

"I'm trying to figure out who our *friend* here really is. She says she's on our side, but if that's true, then why is she wearing a shirt from 4E Labs?"

"What?" Kari gaped at Mile High, who closed her eyes tight as though gathering her thoughts.

Mile High let out a long breath and opened her eyes. She pulled open her jacket and nodded at the logo on her shirt. "It's true. I work at 4E Labs. In the research department."

Recognition dawned on Dylan—Mile High's height, her red hair—she was one of the researchers Mr. Paine had questioned the day they searched 4E Labs looking for Tera after Frank had kidnapped her.

"I knew you looked familiar!" He pointed at her like she was a suspect. "I can't believe I trusted you. I'm so stupid! You've been working for 4E Labs this whole time!" A small part of Dylan's brain told him to take off, but a much larger part—the part that raged with anger—glued his feet in place to stand his ground.

"Please, let me explain." Mile High's voice was even and calm, which outraged Dylan even more.

"I've been working at 4E Labs undercover, trying to figure out why they want the crystals and who is behind the operation."

"And what have you discovered?" Kari asked.

Mile High's shoulders slumped. "Not much. Everyone I asked claimed they didn't know anything. And there was never a record of anyone named Frank associated with the company."

"Frank said he was a 'consultant,'" Dylan pointed out. "He was probably paid cash so there wouldn't be a paper trail." Dylan almost laughed at how much he sounded like a detective from a cop show.

"What if 4E Labs doesn't have anything to do with the crystals?" Kari said. "They could be totally innocent, and that's why nobody has been able to prove anything. It makes sense. Don't you think, Dylan?"

"Yeah, maybe." Even as he said the words, he didn't believe them. Deep in the very pit of his stomach, he knew 4E Labs was involved. He felt it every time he saw that logo—when he first found the business card in the creek, when he saw it on the side of Frank's van, and especially now seeing it on Mile High's shirt. She was a liar and a phony. Even her red hair looked fake, like it had been dyed. Frank could have told her all about the Paines. He was there when Tera's mom died. And Frank certainly could have told her Tera was the catalyst. There was only one way to know for sure if she was telling the truth.

Dylan pulled his phone out of his pocket.

"Who are you calling?" Kari asked.

"I'm texting Tera." Dylan's thumbs typed as he talked. "I want Mr. Paine to confirm the story."

WE HAVE MILE HIGH. NEED YOUR DAD TO COME TO CREEK. NOW.

Mile High stepped toward Dylan. "I don't blame you for not believing me, but I promise it's true."

"Dylan, aren't you overreacting just a little?" Kari said.

"No. Maybe. So what? This whole thing is crazy, and I don't know what to think or who to believe anymore." He scowled at his phone. Why wasn't Tera texting him back?

"So if 4E Labs isn't after the crystals, are there other possibilities for who it could be?" Kari approached Mile High like she was talking to a friend.

"It could be anyone who has ties to the company—a

relative or a friend. Or even an investor."

Dylan looked up from his phone. "If 4E Labs wasn't involved, then how did Frank get a hold of a company van?"

Kari gave him a know-it-all look. "He could have stolen it."

Dylan shook his head. "Mr. Paine said the company never reported a stolen van."

"Then maybe he had the company logo painted on his own van," Kari said.

"Why would he lie about working for 4E Labs? That doesn't make any sense." Dylan wasn't going to let Kari win this argument. He was convinced 4E Labs was somehow involved.

"Frank is a dead end; sorry about the bad pun," Mile High said. "I'm more interested now in why someone wants all four crystals."

"To make the creation stone," Dylan mumbled.

Mile High and Kari turned their heads and stared at him.

"You know about the creation stone?" Mile High asked.

"Yeah. Mr. Lyman told me about it when he showed me the book about the four elements."

"Your neighbor, Mr. Lyman, he's a geologist?"

Dylan nodded.

"Who did he work for before he retired?" Mile High asked.

Dylan shrugged. "I don't know. I never asked." It had never seemed important before.

Mile High frowned. "And he knows about the crystals?"

"I had to tell him." Dylan suddenly realized what Mile High was hinting at. "Hey, Mr. Lyman's a good guy. What, you think he hired someone to break into his own house?"

"No, but maybe he's involved with the wrong people. He's a scientist, and I'm sure the geological community is pretty small. The crystal was at his house. Someone could have come over and seen it, or he might have told somebody about it. I think I need to meet your neighbor."

"No way." Dylan knew Mr. Lyman didn't have anything to do with this, and after the whole car accident, he wasn't about to involve him in any way. "He just got home from the hospital today. It's bad enough I have to tell him about the break-in. I'm not going to let you accuse him of helping the enemy."

Mile High gave him a look of pity. "That's not my intention."

"Mr. Lyman knows a lot about this creation stone stuff," Kari said. "I think you should let her talk to him."

Dylan paced along the creek bank, shaking his head. Why were they ganging up on him? This wasn't how this was supposed to go. He looked at the necklace in his hand. He had the wind crystal, why not just walk away? And where was Mr. Paine?

A gust of wind blew through the creek, ruffling Dylan's hair. He flashed back to the dust devil that had caused the car accident and the image of Mr. Lyman slumped over the steering wheel with blood trickling down his face. It was all because of the wind crystal. The crystal 4E Labs was still after. The crystal Dylan clutched in his hand.

None of this would end until he had answers about

what the crystals could do and why 4E Labs wanted them. And Mr. Lyman might be able to help them figure that out. He sure seemed to know a lot about rocks. Dylan had already told him a little and he wanted to tell him more. Maybe having Mile High talk to Mr. Lyman wasn't such a bad idea after all.

"Okay." Dylan turned around and faced them. "Let's go talk to Mr. Lyman." He walked past them out of the creek and through his back yard, not bothering to check if they were following him. As he made his way down the sidewalk to Mr. Lyman's house, he texted Tera.

CHANGE OF PLANS. HAVE YOUR DAD MEET US AT MR LYMAN'S.

Dylan hoped Tera would get this message, and Mr. Paine would show up to confront Mile High.

When they reached his neighbor's house, Dylan rang the doorbell. As he waited, Mile High and Kari joined him on the porch. It took Mr. Lyman several minutes to answer the door.

"Hello Dylan…and friends." Mr. Lyman smiled but seemed confused by the group.

"Sorry to bother you, Mr. Lyman, but I have someone who wanted to meet you. This is…" Dylan looked at Mile High. He had no idea what her real name was.

Mile High extended her arm toward Mr. Lyman. "I'm Jessica. A friend of Dylan's with a shared interest in the elemental crystals."

Mr. Lyman shook her hand. "I see. Won't you all come in?" He held the door open and stepped aside.

Dylan waited to go in last. "Mr. Lyman? There's something I need to tell you—about your rocks—."

Mr. Lyman patted him on the shoulder. "Not to

worry. We can talk about that later."

"No, I didn't...somebody else..." Dylan didn't want Mr. Lyman to think he had taken the rocks out of the display case, but his neighbor moved into the living room before he had a chance to explain.

"May I offer anyone some lemonade?" Mr. Lyman asked.

"I'd love some. Thank you," Jessica said.

As Mr. Lyman went into the kitchen, Dylan made his way into the living room and sat down on the couch beside Kari. Jessica sat across from them in a straight-backed wicker chair.

Kari leaned toward Dylan. "I thought you said someone stole all of Mr. Lyman's rocks?" she whispered.

"They did." Dylan had avoided looking at the display case out of guilt from the minute he walked into the room.

"Then why is the cabinet full of rocks?" Kari asked.

Dylan glanced at it. Every stone was back in place.

Chapter Twenty-One

Dylan sprang off the couch and stood inches from the display case with his nose almost touching the glass. Every rock was there, including the fake crystal.

"Here we are, fresh lemonade." Mr. Lyman set a tray of filled glasses on the round coffee table in the middle of the room.

"Mr. Lyman, when did you get your rocks back?" Dylan asked.

"The police retrieved them out of the trunk of my car and were kind enough to return them."

"Police?" Had Tera called the cops after Dylan told her about the break-in?

"I had the rocks in my car because I was supposed to display them at a geology expo over the weekend. Apparently Mother Nature had different plans for me." Mr. Lyman smiled and handed Dylan a glass of lemonade.

Dylan sat back down beside Kari and took a sip to hide his embarrassment at being wrong about the theft. But how was he supposed to know? Anyone could have made the same mistake.

Mr. Lyman settled into his desk chair. "Now, Miss… Jessica. How can I be of help?"

Mile High scooted forward on the chair. "Dylan said you know about the crystals. He has the earth crystal, and now he has the wind crystal too."

Mr. Lyman turned his attention to Dylan, who nodded and pulled the necklace out of his pocket. He handed it to Mr. Lyman.

"See the yellow triangle in the middle? That's the wind symbol," Dylan pointed out.

Mr. Lyman picked up a magnifying glass off his desk and examined the crystal. "So it is."

A loud rattle echoed from the kitchen, and Dylan flinched.

"Must be getting windy outside," Mr. Lyman said. "I opened a window to let in some fresh air." He glanced toward the kitchen then back at the wind crystal. He opened his mouth as if to say something, closed it, then opened it again. "So what can I do for you?"

"We're trying to figure out what someone might want the elemental stones for," Mile High said. "What exactly can the creation stone do?"

Mr. Lyman set down the magnifying glass and leaned back in his chair. "I'm no alchemist, but from a geologist's perspective the one thing the creation stone was believed to do was turn base metals into gold and silver. If you can do that, you can make a fortune."

"But what about being able to control the elements?" Kari asked. "Like creating earthquakes and tornadoes and stuff."

Dylan shot her a glare. He hadn't told Mr. Lyman all that yet.

"Then you're talking about more than just greed," Mr. Lyman said. "You're talking about power. And history tells us that those who want power will do anything to get it, at any cost. That's not the kind of thing you kids should get involved with. Isn't that right, Jessica?"

"Yes, that's right." Mile High's cheeks turned the same color as her hair.

Mr. Lyman slid the crystal toward Dylan. "I'm sure you have a good reason for this quest you're on to find all four crystals. And I'm happy to help in any way I can. But I don't think you should keep the stones at your house. There must be somebody else you can entrust them with."

Dylan looked at everyone in the room, and it was obvious to him who that person was. "You're right. There is someone. And I think they should have both crystals. I'll be right back." Without saying anything else he walked out the front door.

A strong breeze blew against him as he sprinted down the street to his house. He glanced at the cotton ball clouds racing overhead. It reminded Dylan a little too much of the day of the car accident, but Tera hadn't been anywhere near the wind crystal today. Was something, or someone, else causing all this weird weather?

He shook off the thought as he ran into his house and took the stairs two at a time up to his room. The earth crystal was still hidden in the Lego house, and Dylan didn't slow down, knocking a few Lego pieces off the shelf in the process. Holding the golf-ball sized crystal in his hand confirmed his decision—it was time to hand this thing over to someone else.

Dylan ran back out of his house so fast he almost tackled Tera, who stood on his front porch.

"Geez, what are you doing here?" He shoved the crystal into his pocket before she could see it in his hand. She'd freak out if she knew how close she was to touching it. "Why didn't you text me back?"

"Sorry. My dad turns off my phone while I do homework. I saw you come home and wanted to talk to you. Why are you in such a hurry?"

Dylan shifted his weight. He wanted to get back to Mr. Lyman's and get the crystal away from Tera. "Mile High is still at Mr. Lyman's house. Where is your dad?"

"He left a few minutes ago. I told him to meet you at Mr. Lyman's once I finally saw your text. I thought that's why you came home. Because my dad had shown up and taken over."

Dylan looked down the street at his neighbor's house, his heart in a panic. "He must be down there right now. I have to go."

"Wait!" Tera ran up behind him. "Who is Mile High? Does he work for 4E Labs?"

"Mile High is a lady. And yeah, technically she works for 4E Labs."

Tera's mouth dropped open.

"But she's on our side. She's trying to figure out why 4E Labs wants the crystals too."

"Who is she?" Tera breathed.

Dylan hesitated to answer. "Her real name's Jessica something. She knows your parents."

"I don't know anyone named Jessica and never heard my dad mention her. I'm coming with you. I want to meet her."

"No! You can't. The crystals are there. You can't get near them." Dylan stuck his hand in his pocket and gripped the crystal like he was creating a barrier between it and Tera.

"If Mile High knew my mom, then I want to talk to

her. Maybe she can tell me more about being a catalyst." Tera looked so hopeful.

Another gust of wind kicked up in Dylan's face like a warning. He couldn't bring Tera to Mr. Lyman's. She was already too close to it and was probably causing all this wind. "Now that we know who Mile High is, I'm sure if you ask your dad he'll let you talk to Jessica sometime, but not now."

Tera grabbed his arm. "Please, Dylan."

A tingling sensation shot down Dylan's arm where Tera had touched it. The crystal warmed in his hand, and he dropped it inside his pocket like a hot coal.

Tera let go of his arm. "What's wrong? You look really freaked out all of a sudden."

Dylan didn't want to scare her by saying he thought she just activated the earth crystal. "I really need to get back to Mr. Lyman's. I'll fill you in on everything that happens. I promise."

Tera's arms fell to her sides, and she looked like a little kid who had just dropped her entire ice cream cone on the ground.

Dylan ran down the street to Mr. Lyman's house and walked in the front door without knocking. All heads turned in his direction. Kari, Jessica, and Mr. Lyman were still in their same seats.

Mr. Paine stood in front of the display case like a teacher in front of a class room. "Dylan, we were just talking about you. It sounds like you've been busy." His voice had a hint of disappointment.

"I'm sorry, Mr. Paine. It all kinda happened really fast." Dylan wanted to say that it had been Tera's idea to hide the earth crystal from her dad, but he didn't want to get her in trouble. "We found another crystal though." He glanced at the desk. The wind crystal still sat in front of Mr. Lyman. Dylan pulled the earth crystal out of his pocket and set it next to the wind crystal.

Mr. Paine's eyes narrowed. "Is that what I think it is?"

"Richard, it's okay." Jessica's voice was soft but full of authority.

Mr. Paine didn't look at her. He didn't say anything else, but a scowl remained on his face.

Dylan took a deep breath. "I want Mr. Lyman to have both crystals. He can keep them safe. And if the crystals are safe, then Tera's safe."

"Now wait a minute—" Mr. Paine stepped toward the desk.

"I think it's a good idea," Jessica interrupted. "They'll be easier to track this way, and 4E Labs won't suspect a thing." She didn't take her eyes off Mr. Paine.

"I'll keep them secure and won't show them to anyone." Mr. Lyman patted the crystals.

Mr. Paine turned his attention to Dylan. "I'll agree if you promise not to go after any more crystals."

Dylan's hopes fell. How could Mr. Paine honestly ask him to do that?

"At least, not without me," Mr. Paine added.

Dylan smiled. "Deal."

Mr. Paine shook Dylan's hand, but his expression changed to concern. "Tera," he whispered.

Dylan turned around. Tera stood on Mr. Lyman's front porch. "What's she doing here? I told her not to come. I promised you'd tell her about Jessica when you got back."

Mr. Paine looked outraged. "You told Tera who Mile High was?"

Dylan cowered below the captain. "Well, yeah. It was the only way I could keep her from coming down here and being near the crystals."

The doorbell rang.

With a few long strides, Mr. Paine reached the front door and met Tera outside. Dylan heard their voices rising and falling. They were definitely arguing.

"You never tell me anything! I have a right to know!" Tera yelled.

Mr. Paine's body blocked the doorway. "You need to go home and wait for me there. It's not safe for you in there."

"I'm not going to go near those stupid rocks. I just want to talk to her."

"I said no, and that's final."

Tera and Mr. Paine didn't move. She stamped her foot and finally turned. Mr. Paine put a hand on the door handle, and as he opened it, Tera spun around. She ducked under her dad's arm and ran inside.

"Tera Paine!" her dad thundered.

Dylan was so shocked, he froze as Tera barged past him into Mr. Lyman's living room.

"Where is she?" Tera looked around the room.

That's when Dylan realized Mile High was gone. And so were the crystals from the desk.

Chapter Twenty-Two

Dylan looked at Mr. Lyman and Kari, waiting for one of them to explain what happened to Mile High and the crystals.

"Where is this Jessica person? Dylan said she was here." Tera gave him a quick glare.

"She was," Kari said. "But then she just jumped up, grabbed the crystals from the desk, and ran through the kitchen."

"She must have gone out the back door," Mr. Lyman added.

"Why?" Dylan asked even though he knew the answer.

"Obviously to keep Tera away from the crystals." Mr. Paine's voice came from behind Dylan.

Tera's jaw tightened when she saw her dad, and in the next instant, she ran to the kitchen. Seconds later a slamming door rattled the house.

"I think Tera just went after Jessica," Kari said.

"Oh man." Dylan didn't even bother waiting for Mr. Paine's reaction before running after Tera. When he reached the door that led out of Mr. Lyman's kitchen and into the back yard, Kari had joined him.

"What are you doing? We don't need to both chase Tera," he said.

"I'm faster than you. I'll go after Jessica and the crystals, you go after Tera."

Dylan wanted to argue, but Kari was right. He'd never be able to catch up to Mile High, and Tera was more important anyway.

Mr. Lyman's back yard was surrounded by a chain link fence, and the gate leading to the front yard was open. Dylan and Kari ran to the driveway and stopped, looking up and down the street.

"There!" Dylan caught a glimpse of Tera's Gatorade-green T-shirt as she darted between houses across the street. "I think she's headed for the creek." He ran in her direction.

"I'll cut through here and see if I can spot Jessica!" Kari called.

Dylan sprinted toward his house then down his back yard and into the creek. He scanned the creek bank but didn't see Tera anywhere. Where did she go? Another gust of wind sent leaves from the nearby trees raining down. He glanced at the sky. Clouds drove in, skidding to a halt and piling up like a traffic jam. It didn't seem natural. Tera must be close to the wind crystal.

Dylan weaved around trees, making his way down the creek. Had Tera crossed the water and climbed up the other bank? The creek was low enough for her to do that. And where was Kari?

"I should have known you'd follow me."

Dylan spun around and faced Tera. "You can't just take off like that."

"Why not? She did. And she took the crystals too." Tera's voice was full of contempt.

"She took them to keep you safe. That's what

everyone is trying to do."

Tera fidgeted with her hands. "I don't care about the crystals. I just wanted to talk to her about my mom."

Dylan didn't know what to say. "Maybe your dad would invite her over, and you could talk."

"Yeah. Maybe." The wind drowned Tera's voice. Her dark hair blew back from her face. Suddenly other voices echoed between the breeze.

Dylan turned his attention to the far side of the creek. He recognized Jessica's red jacket. A tree blocked his view of the person she was talking to, but he was pretty sure it was Kari.

Tera followed his gaze. "Is that her?"

Dylan barely nodded when Tera leapt into the creek, high-stepping through the knee-deep water. "Wait! What are you doing?" He groaned at the thought of following her and debated about taking off his shoes. It'd waste too much time. Instead he stepped into the murky water with one foot. The sole of his shoe settled into the soft bottom as water seeped into his sock. He grimaced but placed his other foot in, then took large steps, hurrying through the cool water.

When Dylan reached the other side, Tera was with Kari, but Jessica had disappeared. Again.

"Why did you let her go?" Tera yelled.

"It's not like I could pin her to the ground!" Kari said.

"What were you two talking about?" Tera demanded.

Kari crossed her arms in front of her. "If you must know, I told her you wanted to talk to her about your mom."

Tera's face softened. "What did she say?"

"She said she wanted to check with your dad first."

Dylan butted between them. "What about the crystals? Is she going to give them to Mr. Lyman?"

Kari gave a sly smile. "Nope."

"What do you mean 'no'? That was the plan! We agreed!" Dylan should have known he couldn't trust her.

"She's not going to give them to Mr. Lyman because she gave them to me." Kari opened her hand to reveal the earth and wind crystals. Their green and gold colored centers glittered in the one patch of sunlight that remained in the sky as the wind whipped leaves up from the ground and sent them swirling.

Tera took a few steps backwards. "I better keep my distance. The wind's been getting stronger the closer I get."

"Here, Dylan. You take them and give them to Mr. Lyman." Kari reached out her arm and dropped the crystals into Dylan's hand.

Right away he noticed a difference between the two rocks. The earth crystal's smooth surface felt cool, but the wind crystal felt like it had been sitting in the sun. It was the same warm sensation he felt when Tera had activated the earth crystal earlier, but this time she hadn't touched the wind crystal. Could she activate it without actually holding it?

"It looks like Mile High's long gone," Tera said. "I'm going back home and having a talk with my dad. He has some explaining to do."

"I guess I'll go give these to Mr. Lyman." Dylan nodded toward the crystals.

"Talk to you guys later." Tera turned and walked right back through the creek water.

Dylan wanted to avoid the muck. "I'm taking the long way around." He walked along the length of the creek bank.

"I'll come with you." Kari followed. They kept silent as they walked, the wind howling through the trees, forcing them to lean forward against its force, their eyes squinted and watering.

Leaves barreled at them, slapping their faces as dirt and dust peppered their eyes. Dylan tried protecting his face with his arm, barely able to see where he was going. He turned around so his back was to the wind. Kari's head was bent low. It didn't look like she was even moving.

"Do you need help?" Dylan yelled but couldn't hear his own words. He cupped his hands around his mouth. "Kari!"

She didn't look up, and the wind whipped her hair across her face, covering it so she looked like a sheepdog. Kari staggered sideways and stopped beside a tree, hugging it for support.

Dylan moved toward her, the wind pushing against his back so he had to slow himself down. "Hold onto me!"

Kari squinted at him through her hair. "What?" she mouthed.

"Take my hand!" Dylan said. When Kari didn't move, he reached out and clasped Kari's hand, then turned around to face the wind again. He took a few steps, tugging Kari behind him. Each step felt like a brick was strapped to his leg.

Kari stayed close, and Dylan knew she was using him to block the wind, but acting as one person made it easier to move against the gusts.

"We need to get out of the creek," she yelled over his shoulder. "Too much stuff flying around!"

Dylan nodded and decided to head up the hill that led out of the creek and to the next block over from their street. The wind seemed to change directions with them, continuing to hammer them head-on.

A violent gust pushed Dylan back so hard he lost his footing and stumbled backward into Kari. Her hand slipped from his, but before he could grab hold again, she fell flat on her back. As soon as her body hit the ground she rolled like a little kid down a grassy hill. Dylan thought she was going to roll right into the creek water, but she stopped when her head smacked against a boulder near the bank. He waited for her to get up, but she laid on the ground face-up like a sunbather.

"Kari!" Dylan skidded down the hill, slipping on the piles of leaves that had collected on the ground from the wind storm. He slid onto his knees next to her and gave her arm a gentle shake. "Can you hear me? Are you okay?" Her eyes stayed closed, and she didn't move. Dylan leaned over to look at the other side of her head. He didn't notice any blood, but she could have had a big bump on the back of her head from hitting the rock. He needed to get her out of there, but carrying her wasn't an option. He reached into his pocket for his phone, but it wasn't there. The only thing in his other pocket were the crystals. His phone must have fallen out when he slid down the hill. Dylan let out a groan. He needed to get help, but he wasn't about to leave Kari in this storm.

Panic crept into Dylan's chest, and his eyes watered even more from the combination of wind and fear. The creek water sprayed over the bank, splashing Dylan and Kari. He tried scooting her away from it, but her limp body was so heavy it didn't do much good. When the wind touched the wet spots of his arms and legs it was like rubbing ice cubes on his body, and he broke out in chills. At least it wasn't pouring rain.

Dylan thought if he could drag Kari away from the creek and under the shelter of a tree, maybe they could wait out the wind storm and then he could get help. He stood up and caught a glimpse of the sky. It had grown darker, a solid wall of clouds from the ground up, tinted a greenish-grey hue. It looked like something out of a Marvel Comics movie. He half expected Thor to come shooting through the clouds, bolts of lightning trailing behind.

In the distance a high-pitched sound wailed, growing steadily louder. Dylan stiffened. It wasn't a sound they heard often in Castle Pines, but he recognized it. Tornado sirens.

Chapter Twenty-Three

Dylan didn't wait for the sirens to blare a second time. He leaned over Kari and placed his hands under her arm pits, lifting her upper body off the ground as he dragged her backwards through the leaves. It was a long way up the hill, but he didn't have time to stop for breaks. The safety procedures for a tornado flashed through is mind. *If outdoors, get to a low lying area and cover your head. Avoid areas where debris is likely. They were in a low lying area, but all these trees made debris very likely.* A branch could easily turn into a flying arrow. Dylan had to get Kari to one of the neighboring houses.

He hadn't gone far when raindrops started pelting him in the face. Within seconds, a wave of water blew sideways, drenching them. Kari's wet arms became slippery, and Dylan's hands lost their grip. The ground turned into slick mud, and his shoes lost all traction. There was no way he could pull Kari up the hill to safety.

"Wake up! You have to wake up!" he yelled above the roaring wind and rain.

She moved her head from side to side but didn't open her eyes.

Dylan patted her cheeks. "Kari! We have to hurry! There's a tornado coming!"

Her eyelids fluttered then closed against the rain.

She put a hand to the back of her head.

"You hit your head on a rock, but you have to get up!" Dylan screamed.

Kari rolled onto her side and tried pushing against the ground to a sitting position. Her hand slipped in the mud and she fell back down on her side. Dylan grabbed her arm to help her up again. Once she sat up, he hoisted her onto her feet.

"Can you walk?" he yelled into her ear.

She nodded and let Dylan turn her around, pointing her in the direction that led up the hill and out of the creek. With heads bent down and arms protecting their faces from the driving rain, they staggered up the hill, their feet sliding along the ground. With every step forward, the wind and rain drove them a few steps back. It seemed like they'd never make it out of the creek.

On the steepest part of the hill, Kari fell to her knees beside Dylan. He grabbed her shoulders and tried lifting her up again.

She shook her head and squinted up at him through the rain. "Let's just wait it out!"

The sirens blared through the wind again, reminding Dylan of the danger. "No way! We're almost there! You can make it!"

"If we lay flat against the ground we'll be okay!"

"Can't you hear the sirens? A tornado is coming!" Why didn't Kari realize this?

"We're not going to get caught in a tornado!"

Dylan shut his eyes against the wind, rain, and Kari's logic. Why was she trying to boss him around at a time like this? Couldn't she just listen to him for once? This time he wasn't going to back down. "We're getting out of here!" He pulled her up by the arm with a little more force than he meant to and wrapped his arm around her waist to support her. She didn't resist, and he half dragged, half carried, her the rest of the way up the hill.

They reached the edge of the trees and exited the creek between two houses. They looked up and stopped. A black spinning funnel cloud hovered directly ahead of them.

The twister danced like a snake on its tail. It slithered between the houses, snapping a few shingles off the roofs but leaving the rest of the house untouched. Chunks of debris swirled in its cloudy mass before being spat back out.

Dylan backpedaled, unable to focus on anything but the giant tornado overhead. "Back to the creek!" he shouted, his voice swallowed by the roar of the twister. He and Kari turned around, running full speed back down the hill. Dylan looked over his shoulder and screamed. The tornado chased them, the tip of its funnel nipping at their heels. The twister's force pushed Dylan forward. He fell into Kari, and they slid down the hill like it was a Slip n' Slide. Dylan skidded to a stop, curled into a ball, and covered his head with his hands, waiting for the tornado to pluck him off the ground and fling him through the air. He hoped he would survive the landing and not end up splattered on someone's driveway. His thoughts jumped to Tera, wondering if she made it home before the storm, hoping she was safe. What about his parents and Jordan? They were probably freaking out not knowing where Dylan was. Where had Mile High gone? Did she have a car parked on another block somewhere? And poor Mr. Lyman. He had been in a car accident only to come home and get caught in a tornado. This definitely wasn't his week.

Dylan waited what seemed like forever. The tornado's roar still deafened his ears, and wind battered against his huddled body, but he hadn't left the ground. He turned his head to the side and peeked under his right arm. Kari wasn't beside him. He turned his head and looked to his left. She wasn't there either. When he didn't see her directly in front of him he scooted in a half circle and finally spotted her several feet behind him. She was kneeling on the ground, sitting back on her heels. Her eyes were squeezed shut and her hands balled into fists in front of her face. The tornado hovered above her head like an exclamation point. It shimmied from side to side and dipped up and down but never touched her. Kari's face scrunched tight, as her wet hair fell limp and a few strands stuck to her cheeks.

Why isn't the wind whipping it around her face? Dylan thought. Then he noticed the rain seemed to avoid her. It was like she was in an invisible bubble.

Dylan didn't move, afraid to mess things up. Was the twister playing with her, waiting to strike? Or was Kari somehow controlling the tornado, keeping it from sweeping over them?

Kari's eyes popped open, and the twister shot up into the clouds like a yo-yo bouncing back on its string. She stared at Dylan, but he didn't think she was really looking at him.

"Kari? Are you okay?" He crawled toward her and waved a hand in front of her face.

Her faraway look finally focused in on him. "Huh?"

"What just happened? Did you make the tornado go

away like that?"

"I…I think so." She looked up toward the sky, which had lightened to pale gray. The rain stopped and the wind calmed.

"How?" Dylan whispered.

Kari's gaze slowly returned to him. "I asked it to."

"You asked the tornado to go away?"

Kari nodded. "Yeah. I said, 'please don't hurt us. Just go back where you came from.' And I guess it did."

Now Dylan glanced at the sky. "Yeah. I guess it did too."

"Dylan?"

He met her eyes. "Yeah?"

"I don't think Tera's the catalyst for the wind crystal."

Dylan gave a slight smile. "I don't think she is either."

"I knew Tera could start earthquakes, but has she ever said anything about controlling them?" Kari looked at her open palms.

"I don't think so." Dylan was pretty sure if Tera knew she could control earthquakes, she would have stopped the one in the mine. "Maybe she can't control them. What if that's something only you can do? With tornadoes, I mean."

"But I'm not sure how I did it, or if I could ever do it again." Kari's eyes focused on Dylan. "Give me the wind crystal."

"Why?" Dylan said slowly. He knew that look. Kari had some crazy idea brewing.

"I want to start another tornado and see if I can make it stop again."

She was definitely crazy. "I think that bump on the back of your head has messed up your brain." There was no way he was going to let her start another tornado. "I'm drenched, cold, and I want to go home."

Kari held out her hand. "Come on. Give it to me. I'll keep it small. Like a dust devil."

"Yeah right, and look how good that turned out."

"Dylan, I'm the catalyst. I should get the crystal."

"No." He backed away from her.

Kari lunged forward and grabbed his arm. "I know it's in your pocket. Hand it over."

Dylan shoved his hands in his shorts' pockets and turned his back toward her. "Uh-uh. I'm not letting you do it."

Kari grabbed his wrist and pulled on his arm. Dylan held his hands firmly in place and twisted his waist, trying to block her with his elbows. He felt the earth crystal brush against his knuckles in his left pocket, but he didn't feel the wind crystal necklace. He knew it was there earlier. He had felt it when he looked for his phone.

"Kari, stop! I think I lost it." Kari let go of his arm, and Dylan pulled his pocket inside out. The only thing in it was the earth crystal.

"What? Where did it go?"

"I don't know. I had it before the storm. It must have fallen out. Help me look for it." Dylan scanned the ground, searching back and forth along the creek bank.

Kari walked up the hill and back down. "The crystal could be anywhere. Buried under leaves, stuck on a branch, or even in the water."

Dylan stared at the creek. Maybe he could use one of those sifters for panning gold to find the crystal. Or he could rake all the leaves around the creek and look for the crystal that way. He had to find it. There was no way he just went through all this only to lose the wind crystal.

Kari walked up beside him, bent over, and rested her hands on her knees. "We're not going to find it in this soggy mess, and my head is pounding. Let's just go home. We can come back tomorrow after school."

Dylan's head and shoulders drooped. She was right. There was no point still looking today. Plus, his body felt like Silly Putty. He was done.

Chapter Twenty-Four

Dylan and his friends were gathered in Tera's front yard the next afternoon. They were all still talking about what had happened.

"You're like the tornado whisperer," Tera said.

EJ tossed a football in the air. "I knew there was a reason you're so full of hot air. How about you use your power for good? I could use a tornado drill right about the time we have our math test tomorrow."

Kari rolled her eyes. "Too bad for you. We lost the wind crystal, remember? So it looks like you're going to have to actually study."

Dylan let go of the tree branch he was dangling from and dropped to the ground. They had all searched the creek for an hour after school but hadn't found the crystal.

Tera sat next to Kari on the front porch. "I still can't believe you're a catalyst too. It's just so weird."

"I feel awful that I must have started the dust devil that caused Mr. Lyman's accident," Kari said.

Tera put her arm around Kari. "It wasn't your fault. You know that."

"Yeah, and Mr. Lyman is going to be fine," Dylan added.

"Hey, does that mean one of your parents was a

catalyst?" Tera asked.

"I don't know. I tried bringing it up, but I had no idea what to say. 'Hey Mom, Dad, do either of you have a super power that lets you control tornadoes?' They'd have me committed. I did ask them one thing though—how they came up with the name Kari. They said I was named after my great grandmother. She was from Norway. So I looked up 'Kari' online and guess what? It means 'wind' in Norwegian. Isn't that wild?"

"It's awesome! I knew there was a reason we're best friends," Tera said.

Kari linked her arm through Tera's. "But now you and I aren't just best friends, we're like sisters. Crystal sisters."

Tera giggled. "I've always wanted a sister."

"Sisters are overrated," Dylan mumbled, trying to hide his jealousy now that Kari and Tera were even closer.

"I wonder if we really are related?" Kari asked. "Like distant cousins or something. Wouldn't that be amazing? Our powers could go back for generations!"

"I thought you had to be 13 before your powers kicked in," EJ said. "You don't turn thirteen until Saturday."

Kari shrugged. "My mom always says I'm an overachiever. Speaking of my birthday, you're all coming to my luau, right?"

EJ groaned. "You've already asked us like ten times. Yes, we'll be there!"

"The invitations were so cute," Tera said. "I loved the picture of the hula girls in their grass skirts."

"And I expect everyone to come dressed for a luau.

And I mean *everyone*." Kari looked at the boys.

Dylan didn't know why girls always had to dress up for stuff. Jordan had made a huge deal out of it when she saw the invitation on the kitchen fridge. She wanted him to wear one of her wrap around skirts. It looked like a giant silk scarf covered with tropical fish. And she had suggested a pair of her blingy flip-flops. He wouldn't be caught dead in either one. His swim trunks and a T-shirt were going to have to cut it.

"And don't feel like you have to bring presents," Kari added.

"Don't worry, I wasn't going to," EJ said.

Dylan wondered if that was true. His mom already said they were going shopping after school this week to pick out a present for Kari. His stomach clenched at the thought of shopping for a girl.

"Your parents are welcome to come too. The whole neighborhood is!" Kari spread her arms out wide, her voice echoing off the covered porch

"My dad and I will both be there. I can't wait." Tera nudged Kari with her shoulder.

Dylan joined the girls on the front porch. "Are you going to tell your dad about Kari being a catalyst?"

Tera looked to Kari for an answer.

"It's okay. I don't mind. Especially since the wind crystal is still out there somewhere. It'd be nice to know someone is looking out for me. Hey, did you talk to your dad about Jessica?"

Tera let out a long sigh. "Yeah. He told me how he used to work with her, and she and my mom had become friends. When I asked if I could meet her, he said 'When the time is right.' He babbled on about how it was really important to protect her identity so she could stay undercover at 4E Labs. What, does he think I'm going to expose her or something? Anyway, I tried arguing, but he wasn't going to budge. I did post a message on the blog site Dylan and I used. If I can't meet her, maybe I can at least chat with her."

Dylan thought was a pretty clever idea. "Did she post a message back?"

"Not yet, but I just did it this morning before school. I'll let you know."

"It sounds like we can trust her though, since your dad backed up her story," Kari said.

"And if we have her and Mr. Lyman all helping look for clues about the other two crystals, then we'll have a better chance at finding them." Dylan had a renewed desire to complete his mission.

"You mean three crystals," Kari said. "We have to find the wind crystal. Again."

Dylan wasn't ready to give up on that yet either. He was going to search the creek every day if he had to. It had to be there somewhere.

A maroon colored car drove down the street and pulled into Tera's driveway.

"Who's that?" EJ asked, pointing at the car with his football.

"I think it's Colonel Thornton. My dad said he was stopping by on his way back from his fishing trip for a debriefing."

The colonel got out of his car, wearing jeans and a tan safari shirt with a fishing lure hooked to the pocket. A black messenger bag was slung over his shoulder. "Afternoon, kids."

The girls said hello, Dylan gave a small wave, and EJ mumbled something about having to go get ready for football practice.

"I better go too." Kari stood up and brushed off the back of her shorts. "See you guys later."

Tera stood up and faced Dylan. "Are you leaving?"

Colonel Thornton approached them. "Actually, I was hoping to have a quick word with Dylan. If that's all right?"

Dylan shrugged. "Sure."

"I guess I'll talk to you later then." Tera mouthed 'call me' before heading inside.

Colonel Thornton took a book out of his bag. "I wanted to give this back to you. It was really informative. I'm hoping you can thank Mr. Lyman for letting me borrow it."

Dylan accepted the book. "Oh, yeah. No problem."

"Captain Paine mentioned you found a wind crystal and that it caused quite an ordeal."

Dylan stiffened. Did the colonel know he had lied about the earth crystal too? "It caused Mr. Lyman's car accident."

"I'm glad your neighbor is okay." Colonel Thornton cleared his throat. "I have to say, I think it's rather curious that Mr. Lyman, who happens to be a geologist and the owner of that book, was the one who led you to the wind crystal in the first place. And wasn't he also the one who told you about the cache that led you to Dove Mountain, where you rescued Tera?"

Dylan looked down at the book and ran his hand over the leather cover. What was Colonel Thornton getting at? "Yeah, I guess Mr. Lyman was the one who told me about both of those caches, but that's because he knows I like geocaching. And he's a local cache reviewer so he's one of the first people to find out about them."

"And did you know he's also a shareholder of 4E Labs?" the colonel asked.

Dylan gave him a confused look. "What does that mean?"

"It means he owns a small piece of the company. So if 4E Labs makes money, then its shareholders make money too."

"So…?" Dylan didn't know where the Colonel was going with all this.

"So, if 4E Labs is looking to profit in some way off the crystals, then Mr. Lyman would make money off them too."

Dylan's stomach suddenly felt uneasy, like when he didn't know an answer on a test. "Aren't a lot of people shareholders?"

"Yes, but I doubt many of them have a connection to the crystals like Mr. Lyman does." The colonel gestured toward the book.

Dylan couldn't blame the colonel for wondering if Mr. Lyman might be involved. He had even thought his neighbor was Mile High. But working for the enemy? He just couldn't believe it. Mr. Lyman was too nice. And too old. He had been helping Dylan find the crystals. If Mr. Lyman was after them, he could have gotten the wind crystal all by himself. And he had the earth crystal all that time. He could have easily handed it over to 4E Labs.

"I know you wanted Mr. Lyman to safeguard the crystals, but I think it'd be best if you gave the earth crystal to Captain Paine instead. Let the military do its job." Colonel Thornton patted Dylan's shoulder as he walked by on his way into Tera's house.

Dylan stared back at the book in his hands and headed down the street to Mr. Lyman's. He had to find out if the colonel could be right.

His neighbor was out front watering flowers and waved as Dylan walked into his driveway. "Good to see you, Dylan. What brings you by?"

Dylan held up the book. "Colonel Thornton brought this back and asked me to tell you 'thanks.'"

Mr. Lyman set down his watering can and took the book. "I hope it was helpful."

"He said it was. Now we have a bunch of people looking for the other crystals. I just wish I hadn't lost the wind crystal in the creek."

"At least you still have the earth crystal," Mr. Lyman said.

"Yeah, about that. I guess Mr. Paine's going to keep it from now on. Colonel Thornton's orders."

Mr. Lyman nodded. "I see."

"And, I hate to ask this, but that other crystal, the fake one I gave you? Well, it was a gift, and if you don't mind, I'd kind of like it back." If Dylan had to give up the real earth crystal, then at least he wanted to hang on to the one Tera had given him.

"No problem, Dylan. I understand. Let me go inside and get it for you."

Dylan waited as Mr. Lyman slowly made his way into the house. He didn't look like someone who could be part of a plot to kidnap Tera and gain control over powerful crystals.

Mr. Lyman came out a few minutes later. "Here you are." He handed Dylan the rock.

"Thanks." Dylan slid it into his shorts pocket. "Mr. Lyman? You'll tell me if you see any more caches posted online that might have to do with one of the crystals, won't you?"

The lines around Mr. Lyman's soft blue eyes grew longer as he smiled. "Dylan, consider us partners in crime."

Chapter Twenty-Five

Dylan stood on Tera's front porch waiting for her to answer the door. He fidgeted with the pink ribbon wrapped around Kari's birthday present. He glanced down at the black flip-flops his mom had bought him, hoping they didn't look too silly with his neon green swim trunks and orange T-shirt. He didn't know if it was what they wore at luaus, but at least they were bright colors.

Tera answered the door, looking like she had just stepped off Kari's invitation. She wore a colorful floral sundress that tied behind her neck. A grass skirt that matched her green eyes was wrapped around her waist. Her long dark hair was pulled back on one side with a red flower tucked behind her ear.

"Wow. You look…great." Dylan thought maybe he should have listened to his sister's fashion advice after all.

"Thanks. You do too." Tera had a small wrapped gift in one hand and closed the front door with the other. They walked across the street to Kari's house.

Dylan couldn't help looking at her every few seconds. He had never seen her so dressed up. Every time he wanted to say something, the words sounded dumb in his head. It was like they had just met. He was nervous all over again.

A sign on Kari's front door said "Come In. Party Out Back." When Tera and Dylan reached the back yard they stopped and stared. A giant white tent covered the entire grass area. Lit tiki torches circled the tent, which housed tables draped in floral tablecloths. On each table sat a centerpiece made up of a candle, sand, and seashells. An open fire pit sat in one corner of the patio where a full-sized pig rotated on a metal spit. Guests of all ages mingled, some wearing grass skirts, bright colored Hawaiian shirts, and leis.

Kari ran up to Tera and Dylan. She was dressed like Tera's twin except with a hot pink flower tucked behind her ear instead of a red one. Dylan had never seen her hair in anything other than a messy ponytail. For once she looked like a girl.

"Aloha!" Kari placed a flower lei around each of their necks. A sweet scent shot up Dylan's nose. The leis were made from real flowers.

"The place looks amazing!" Tera squealed.

"Thanks. My parents really went all out. There's punch and snacks in the tent. EJ's already in there of course. Come on." She grabbed Tera's hand and led them to the tent.

Dylan spotted someone hunched over the food table shoveling chips and salsa into their mouth. He had to look twice to believe it was his best friend. EJ wore a tan grass skirt, a blue and white button down Hawaiian shirt, and had a crown of flowers on his head. Only his feet looked normal in bright blue flip-flops.

EJ straightened when he saw his friends. "Say anything, and I'll tackle you."

"What? You look very…Polynesian," Tera giggled.

"My mom made me wear this getup. It's better than what Fish is wearing. Where's your grass skirt?"

Dylan gave EJ a slight shove and grabbed a handful of chips, ignoring the question.

Tera handed Kari her gift. "I know you said no gifts, but I couldn't resist."

Kari grinned and carefully opened the small package. Inside were a pair of silver earrings. One was the letter "K" and the other the letter "T."

"They're friendship earrings, each with our initial," Tera said.

Kari hugged her and put them on, then pointed at Tera. "Hey, you got your diamond earrings back!"

Tera grinned. "My dad took me back to the pawn shop. I owe him the two hundred dollars it took to get them out of hock, but he said I can work it off. He's going to have the cleanest car in Castle Pines for the next year."

"Mine's not quite that good." Dylan handed her his gift. She opened this one just as carefully. "It's a bunch of rolls of colored athletic wrap—pink, purple and stuff. My sister said all the girls wear it for sports."

"We do! Thanks. I can totally use this." Kari gave Dylan a hug and glanced at EJ.

He rolled his eyes and pulled a wadded up plastic bag out of his shorts' pocket underneath his grass skirt. "Here." EJ held it out toward Kari.

She gave him a curious look and opened the bag, then pulled out a long wide piece of pink leather. "Is this a bracelet? It has 'I love soccer' stamped into it."

"My mom's friend makes them," EJ mumbled.

Kari wrapped it around her wrist and snapped it in

place. "It's awesome. Thanks, EJ."

He shrugged. "No big deal."

"Wow, I got earrings, a bracelet, and headbands. All I need now is a necklace. Dylan, any luck finding the wind crystal?"

"Nope. I think it's long gone." Dylan had gone back to the creek every day after school but hadn't found it. He figured the tornado must have sucked it up and carried it off somewhere.

"I forgot to tell you guys, I heard back from Jessica," Tera said. "We set up a private chat online, and we've been having all kinds of conversations. She told me a bunch of stuff about my mom, like that she was a really good artist. I had no idea! She said she has some of my mom's paintings and will send them to me."

Mrs. Johanson walked into the tent. "The pig is ready, if you're hungry."

"That's what I'm talking about!" EJ pushed past them.

"I'm starving," Tera said, following him out of the tent.

"Kari, this was on the kitchen counter, but I don't know who it's from." Mrs. Johanson handed Kari a small square box with a gold ribbon tied around it.

"Thanks, Mom. I'll come eat in a minute."

Mrs. Johanson walked out of the tent, leaving Kari with the gift.

"Open it," Dylan said.

Kari slid off the ribbon and opened the box. She took out a small card and read it out loud. "'To Kari, Happy 13th Birthday.' It's not signed." She flipped the card over, then unwrapped the tissue paper. She gasped before pulling out a long gold chain. On the end of it dangled the wind crystal. She stared at Dylan.

"It's not from me."

"Then who?" Kari asked. She and Dylan walked to the tent opening and looked at the guests. He saw Mr. Paine, but knew he wouldn't give the crystal to Kari. Next he spotted Mr. Lyman talking to Mrs. Johansen, but Dylan doubted his neighbor would have been able to get to the creek to find the crystal. He was still moving slowly after the accident. Then his attention turned to Tera who was in line beside EJ, waiting for the roast pig. He thought of Jessica. Maybe she found the crystal and figured out Kari was the real catalyst. The tent flaps fluttered as a gust of wind blew through.

"I don't know who gave you the crystal, but you better put it back in the box before your entire party blows away."

Kari wrapped her hand around the crystal, and a bright flash of yellow radiated from its triangular center. Then she clasped the chain around her neck.

"What are you doing?" Dylan whispered. Light faded as clouds appeared in the sky, blocking out the sun.

Kari closed her eyes and her lips moved slightly, but her words were too quiet for Dylan to hear. The clouds continued to roll in, and another gust of wind blew through the tent. Dylan wondered if he should try taking the necklace off Kari, but he knew that once a crystal was activated, you couldn't stop it. Or could you?

As Kari kept up her silent chant, Dylan noticed breaks in the billowy clouds. Streams of sunlight broke through, and just as quickly as they had arrived, the clouds vanished. Kari's eyes opened. She looked at the sky and smiled.

"You did it," Dylan said. "You controlled the wind."

"It was easier this time. I said I wanted the clouds to go away, the wind to calm, and the sun to come out. Then it happened."

"This is amazing! Wait until Tera and EJ find out about this." Dylan wanted to run over and tell them. But then he spotted Mr. Paine. "There's just one problem. We're supposed to give the crystals to Tera's dad."

Kari slipped the necklace inside her dress. "We will, just not tonight. I want to hang on to this a little longer."

Dylan nodded. He couldn't blame her for that. Besides, whoever had given Kari the necklace obviously thought she should have it. And he knew how hard it was to give up the crystals. He wasn't ready to hand over the earth crystal to Mr. Paine either. And now that he had the fake one back from Mr. Lyman, he could easily switch them out again—no one would ever have to know.

Dylan and Kari joined EJ and Tera in the food line.

"About time you showed up. I was going to eat your half of the pig." EJ picked up one of the mini tiki torches out of its holders, stepped back, and twirled it like a baton. "Check it out! I'm a fire dancer!"

Kari glared at him. "Egan Doyle, put that down before you set my entire birthday party on fire!"

Dylan laughed, but as he stared at the spinning flame against the cloudless sky, he suddenly knew which crystal cache he was going to search for next.

the end.

About the Author

Kathy Sattem Rygg is the author of *The Crystal Cache* series as well as the author of the Hidden Gem award winning chapter books *Tall Tales with Mr. K* and *TALLER Tales with Mr. K*, and the author of the highly acclaimed middle grade book *Animal Andy*. She has more than 15 years of experience in marketing and public relations, and has held editorial positions for a number of publications. Ms. Rygg is from Omaha, NE, where she lives with her two children and enjoys sharing her love for writing.

About Knowonder

Knowonder is a leading publisher of engaging, daily content that drives literacy; the most important factor in a child's success.

Parents and educators use Knowonder tools and content to promote reading, creativity, and thinking skills in children from zero to thirteen.

Knowonder's products and books deliver original, compelling stories and content, creating an opportunity for parents to connect to their children in ways that significantly improve their children's success.

Ultimately, Knowonder's mission is to eradicate illiteracy and improve education success through content that is affordable, accessible, and effective.

www.knowonder.com